The Book of
OPPOSITES

The Book of
OPPOSITES

JOHN DAVID MORLEY

For John Jones
— Woh! But also Wah! —

Published in 2010 by Max Press
73 Campden Hill Towers, London WII 3QP

10 9 8 7 6 5 4 3 2 1

Text copyright © by John David Morley
Design and layout © by Max Press

A CIP catalogue record for this book is available from the British Library

ISBN 978 1906251 07 9

Printed and bound by Bookmarque, Croydon

CHAPTER
I

Pfrumpy would have been driving. He had driven on the way there, seemed probable he would have been driving on the way back, too. Frank didn't like driving, only drove when he had to, and as neither he nor Pfrumpy felt comfortable with Wilma's driving – fretful, said Pfrumpy, inspired though not always, Wilma admitted, while in Frank's opinion it shouldn't have been allowed on the roads – it was usually Pfrumpy who did the driving. He was a good driver. He felt comfortable driving, unwinding the road like it was something that came out of the car, as if it was the car driving there that made the road.

Pfrumpy's car resembled Pfrumpy. A big, heavy car, a solid-core, armour-plated Mercedes 600. Built in the late iron age of the 1970s and originally owned by an industrialist who lived in fear of assassination by terrorists, it was one of the last from the pre-plastic era of automobiles. It must have weighed a ton, perhaps even two. When driven fretfully by Wilma, as on a number of memorable occasions it had been, it could cause major damage to minor cars without – and this particularly annoyed the battered party – the slightest trace of injury to itself.

A murky wet Saturday afternoon in late October, a heavy-lidded sort of day with an almost audible groan – or was it a chuckle? Leaf mould on the ground, death in the air. Unusually chilly for the time of year. The heating in the car was turned on, the fold-in ashtrays fore and aft folded out, steaming with the heating at full blast. So here was the equation giving the freight the car was carrying. One driver + three passengers = (in those days, at any rate) four smokers with a significantly reduced life expectancy.

Figures of speech.

We were on our way to a wedding outside Potsdam, at least, they were. I was going to see my supervisor, who lived in Potsdam, and they dropped me off on the way.

It was an acquaintance of Wilma's who was getting married, Nick the Greek, Wilma loved weddings, and particularly Coptic Greek ones, in advance of knowing what they were like, for she had never been to a Greek wedding, Coptic or otherwise. Frank and Pfrumpy tagged along to keep her company, would have tagged along even if Wilma had been going to a Greek funeral – perhaps rather more happily to the funeral. Frank actually detested weddings and preferred, or claimed to prefer, it may just have been a pose, funerals.

Pfrumpy reserved judgement. Knowing Pfrumpy, he had no urgent opinion on this matter either way.

The traffic was unusually heavy that afternoon. It took us over an hour to get from Pfrumpy's house in downtown Berlin to Berlin-Zehlendorf. Wilma repeatedly came up with cunning shortcuts, probably saving us a lot more time. She may not have been much as a driver, but she was a great navigator.

After three years in Berlin, Wilma knew her way around the city incredibly well, not just to get from A to B. Given the nature of her work, prying around and poking her nose into dark corners all over the place, she had in fact got to know Berlin a lot better than many Berliners. The locals tended to stick to their own turf and take little interest in other people's. Ten years after the Wall, there would be people living in West Berlin who still hadn't bothered to make a trip to the eastern part of the city and check out what, if anything – and anything can only have been noted with a shudder of interest – they had been missing all those years.

Nightfall was coming on when we reached the bridge. The road rose like a white scar in the gloom of the trees in the surrounding park. There is a slight incline with a cobbled surface on the approaches at either end of the bridge. It can be tricky to negotiate when covered with wet leaves. Crossing the bridge over the Havel, which at this point widens out into a lake, you pass from Berlin to Potsdam. It is one of the scenic spots in the region.

During the Cold War, Glienicker Bridge also used to mark the frontier between East and West. Under exceptional circumstances, such as the exchange of spies – *Kundschafter*, 'scouts', was the official terminology sanctioned in the East – the bridge was opened a few times for crossing from Potsdam to Berlin, but otherwise, unlike the official transit point at Checkpoint Charlie, it remained closed to traffic for more than a quarter of a century.

Maintenance work on Glienicker Bridge, particularly the section in the middle where the border ran, had been more or less neglected for as long as the bridge remained closed. There were calls from public-minded people for it to be closed again. But closing the bridge just after it had been opened was not a political option. Three years after the fall of the Wall, the job of thoroughly overhauling the bridge had only just begun.

On the cobbled approach to the bridge, probably before the car actually rolled onto it, Wilma seemed to be disturbed by something. A flicker of unease, or what I took to be unease, just a shadow that flitted across her face, was apparently triggered by the giant hoarding she saw on the side of the road.

She drew our attention to it. We all looked.

The hoarding was still there, two years after the elections which had been the reason for putting it up in the first place. It would remain there for several years more, unlike the old sign that read YOU ARE LEAVING THE AMERICAN SECTOR, which had been dismantled immediately after the Wall came down. Its continued presence served as a reminder that people in the former Eastern sector still hadn't moved beyond the one-people one-party notion that election slogans on paper were commandments carved in granite, approved by the Central Committee, and once such words had got themselves up on a hoarding you didn't just take them down. They were there to stick around for a while.

– Funny, where did that billboard spring from? I never noticed it before. Was it here last time we came? I've read that *slogan*, uhm, well, I don't know, *somewhere*, I mean not here, you know.

Wilma wrung her hands, as she did when agitated, literally: wrung her hands.

— Siebenund — Frank, help me can you?

After three years in Berlin Wilma spoke the language well enough but she still had problems getting those long German words out of her mouth in one piece. Turning to Frank sitting behind her, she asked him to pronounce them for her, having tried and failed to do so convincingly enough to satisfy herself.

— *Siebenundfünfzig Jahre sind genug.*

— Fifty-seven years are enough?

— Right.

— Fifty-seven years of what?

— Well . . .

Frank began to explain.

It was a subject of particular interest to me, which was why I didn't pay too much attention to the road we were travelling. Perhaps I was a bit jealous that Wilma had asked Frank rather than me. After all, I was the expert. I knew much more about it than he did.

We crossed the bridge and I hadn't even registered it, let alone any indication of work in progress on the bridge. There would likely have been road signs saying Work in Progress, but I didn't see them, or if I did I don't remember them.

Frank was still in full spate when the car stopped to let me off at my destination. Once you got Frank started on something it was difficult to stop him. Probably he continued for the rest of the way to the wedding, and perhaps on the way back too. I don't know, of course, for I wasn't in the car when it returned to Berlin the following morning.

Perhaps Frank and Wilma drank too much at the Greek wedding and were fast asleep on the journey home. Not Pfrumpy. He never touched a drink. Pfrumpy would have been driving. But this conjecture is unnecessarily misleading. We know it positively for a fact. Pfrumpy was driving.

CHAPTER
2

Frank was a drifter and came out of nowhere, which in Berlin was generally understood to be the boondocks in the provinces. This may have been the reason why he never talked about where he came from. It may also have had to do with a cool image Frank liked to project, as if he had come into the world without troubling himself with uncool things like parents or the hovel of a provincial home. Apart from the fact that his mother was American, which in an unguarded moment he once let slip, Frank had no known antecedents, seemed to have discarded his entire life prior to surfacing in Potsdamer Platz three and a half months after the fall of the Wall in November 1989.

Our first sighting of Frank has been reliably documented by two witnesses, Tom and Gerrit.[1]

Approaching from opposite directions across Potsdamer Platz on the eastern side of the Wall, which transected the square, the three of them reached the puddle at exactly the same time. The puddle was frozen over. Tom urinated on it; prophetically, it would turn out, although for the moment with no effect beyond creating a slowly spreading pale yellow stain, which he photographed with a Polaroid camera. Armed with a 2-metre long pole, Gerrit proceeded to break the ice while Frank, poleless, looked on.

Gerrit poked the pole into the puddle and found it encountered no resistance. He inserted it half way, then knelt down and pushed it all the way in, and still didn't touch the bottom.

Det wat a pretty deep puddle, reckoned the guttural Dutchman, Gerrit, and Tom, who turned out to be a Londoner, agreed.

Kids' stuff, scoffed Frank, cool.

Ignoring Frank, Tom and Gerrit squatted down for a smoke in the lee of the Wall and kept an eye on the puddle while contemplating their next move.

In the meantime Frank had gone scavenging in the wasteland. Among the rubble of mud and broken masonry he found a coil of wire. Uncoiling the wire, he laid it out on the ground in a straight line, which he measured at fifteen paces. Frank walked back to the puddle, one hand trailing the wire behind him, the other hand holding a brick.

Watch, he said.

He inserted the wire through a hole in the brick, twisted it round the brick a couple of times, then lowered the brick into the puddle, slowly, hand over hand, a solitary sailor lowering anchor into the depths of the wasteland of Potsdamer Platz. Reaching the end of the wire at fifteen metres he let go, and it immediately sank out of sight.

That was a pretty deep puddle, said Frank quite loudly to himself, without even a glance at the two men smoking in the lee of the Wall. Tom and Gerrit stood corrected.

– Need a pump. Might as well.

Frank delivered himself of this glancing remark in the lofty manner he sometimes adopted, which one can imagine as somewhat like the manner of a mounted Parthian archer discharging an arrow from his bow, en passant over his shoulder, not bothering to look round, confident his bolt had struck its mark, and just bounding off at an obtuse angle, leaving his two co-discoverers of the puddle squatting under the Wall.

Tom and Gerrit were, indeed, still huddled on guard over the puddle when Frank returned three hours later. He was dragging a supermarket trolley, piled high with a variety of articles including a diesel pump, a battery pack, a generator, a 20-litre can of fuel and a coil of wide-gauge hose.

By the time they began pumping water out of the mysterious hole in the ground it was already dark and growing increasingly cold. Too cold for curiosity, they watched without interest a woman taking photographs of them across the square. Frank deployed his troops in various flanking manoeuvres. Quartermaster Gerrit was sent west on recce for food and warm clothing, Private Tom to forage discreetly for firewood in apparently derelict buildings to the east.

Frank himself, warming to his role as sapper, became concerned about the water pumped out of the hole being soaked up by the ground and eventually seeping back into the hole. He had done a spot survey of the terrain and detected a slight falling away of the ground on the far side of the Wall. One section of it had been breached about sixty metres from the puddle, beyond reach of the hose. Before the stores closed he obtained an additional length of hose, directing the flow of water through this breach into a clump of dead trees on the west side of the Wall.

The first night they spent huddled by the bonfire in near freezing temperatures, exposed to the cold easterly wind that swept across Potsdamer Platz. It was a square that had survived only in name, a houseless, treeless wasteland, any vestiges of cover levelled by bulldozers to give East German border guards a clear line of fire.

From time to time someone got up to shine a flashlight and piss into the hole. The water level was going down, but not much. Adding increments of urine served to demonstrate their impatience with its slow progress. Apart from that, they enjoyed the tinkling sound, in which they could hear discrete evidence of themselves in the eerie hollowness below. The state of the puddle temporarily declined in interest as the cold increased. Frank rallied his men, had them march around singing songs to keep warm. Tom and Gerrit went off duty in the middle of the night, returning the next morning with camping equipment, a primus stove, sleeping bags and a tent, in which Frank slept until noon.

When he got up and assessed the situation the water level in the dome-like subterranean space that had opened up beneath last night's puddle seemed hardly any lower than when he had looked at it six hours previously. On the far side of the Wall, however, the hollow with the clump of dead trees had been transformed overnight into a quite impressive lake. The broken tarmac, the antique sidewalk lampposts and weed-filled tram tracks of what had once been a major thoroughfare across Potsdamer Platz, allegedly the busiest square in Europe, now lay submerged beneath an oil-slicked, filth-strewn moat extending half way round the block.

Frank withdrew the hose, switched off the pump and called the fire brigade.

When the fire engines arrived Frank was waiting to meet them on the West side of the Wall, a local resident who had done no more than his duty in informing the responsible civic authority of a potential public hazard. How such quantities of water could have accumulated there so quickly was as much a mystery to Frank as it was to the fire chief.

Whatever the explanation, powerful suction machines disposed of the lake in two shakes, dumping it in mobile tanks and whisking them away. The fire chief ordered the drains under the clump of dead trees by the Wall to be opened. Finding that they were completely blocked, he had them flushed out with a high-pressure hose. The residue of the lake ran off underground with a merry chortling sound that was music to the fire chief's ears no less than it was to Frank's. Nothing had been done to these drains for as long as anyone could remember, the fire chief confided, what else, under the circumstances, could one expect?

When Frank suggested stepping through the Wall into East Berlin to see if the lake on the West side could be traced to an unauthorised leak there the fire chief said emphatically it was no concern of his, the Wall marked the point where West Berlin ended, and where it ended his jurisdiction did too. Just out of curiosity though, he did take a peek. In the former death zone on the other side of the Wall the fire chief saw the encampment of some vagrants who appeared to have made themselves as comfortable as the circumstances allowed, sitting in armchairs drawn round a fire. A woman wearing the chequered headgear of a Palestinian freedom fighter was manoeuvring around them, taking photographs.

Draining the puddle, the *cavernous puddle*, as it had now become known, continued without any major hold-ups for another three days and nights.

On the first of March a mild thaw set in, bringing anarchy in its wake. Bystanders who had just come for a quick look stayed all day.

Some of them, mostly kids, left the site only to return with their own tents and thermal underwear, enabling them to stay there all night too.

On the rim of the cavernous puddle, as the encampment grew, half a dozen bonfires that were dotted around the death zone of Potsdamer Platz lit up the night, in flagrant violation of bylaws relating to unauthorised camping, waste disposal, toilet facilities, noise, smells and other emissions, the consumption of alcohol, open fires in general and the burning of fossil fuels in particular, to name only a few.

No one could have cared less, neither those who broke the laws nor those whose job it was to enforce them, because no one felt responsible for what happened in the no-man's-land on the far side of the Wall, not in West Berlin and in East Berlin least of all, elevating the fire chief's off-the-cuff remark to Frank to a principle that would be tacitly observed for years to come. No one was willing to recognise such a monstrosity as falling within their jurisdiction.

CHAPTER
2.1

On the third day Frank put on a harness and was winched down into the hole. He found himself inside what appeared to be a dome. A smoothly curving wall descended uniformly all around him. Looking down at the black mass of water, although it was only six to eight metres below, Frank felt the familiar prickling gooseflesh down his shins, a prickle of fear, by no means confined to his present situation, Frank once told me, as if to say that he spent much of his life dangling over a virtual abyss that yawned beneath him.

He asked for a hose to be passed down to him so that he could spray the dirt-encrusted surface of the dome. Flaking off the grime, bit by bit he saw patterns emerge under the jet of water, birds in arching branches bordered by floral ornamentation, a spreading peacock, a mottled snake uncoiling in an upward spiral round the dome. The whole thing was beautifully done in a mosaic of blue and white tiles. In his enthusiasm, Frank sent up word that quickly did the rounds, even made it as a headline in the Local section of a reputable newspaper.

'Basilica unearthed beneath Potsdamer Platz?'[2]

At a depth of fifteen metres from the top of the dome the mosaic ended, giving way to rows of vertical white tiles interspersed with rhomboid shapes set crosswise in blue. By this time the seabed of the drowned basilica had been plumbed to a depth of nineteen and a half metres. More powerful suction pumps were required to hoover up a semi-solid, evil-smelling sludge that covered the inlaid marble floor, which in due course was cleaned up and revealed to be in as astonishingly pristine a condition as the rest of the building.

One curious feature that nobody could explain was a convex ledge, twenty-two centimetres deep, one metre from the floor. It ran round the entire chapel-like interior of what was evidently a substantial edifice, with a diameter at floor level of twenty-five meters. Slits in the wall above the ledge at regular intervals along the circumference all the way round the perfectly circular room suggested a water conduit, giving rise to a number of ingenious theories regarding the nature of the rituals that might once have been practised here.

All such speculations were terminated by the publication of a reader's letter[3] in response to the report of the basilica that had allegedly been discovered beneath Potsdamer Platz. It was written by a pensioner who had grown up in the neighbourhood and was employed as a junior clerk by an insurance company on Potsdamer Platz during the late 1920s and early '30s.

In those days, he wrote, in-house plumbing could not be taken for granted by junior clerks as it was today. They were shunted off into annexes without such facilities as running water. He knew the 'basilica' well. On his way to and from and during work he had stepped in there several times a day for the best part of ten years. He had stood inside the Peacock Room, as it used to be known, and unbuttoned his fly alongside the famous physicist Max Planck, the boxer Schmeling, the likes of Goering and Hess before their political apotheosis definitively removed them from public conveniences of any kind.

The sunken chamber Frank had excavated was a pissoir. It was a urinal well-known in its day for the quick lunch-time homosexual rendezvous, and for its extravagant Wilhelminian decor, which in 1900 had been an expression of the imperial ambitions for what was then the fastest growing city in the world.

CHAPTER
2.2

— Then we'll turn it into a disco and call it Pissoir.

They told Frank what a blunder he'd made, what a fool of himself. They thought the laugh was on him. But it didn't faze Frank, not for a second. When they told him what he had excavated was not a basilica but a urinal he came straight back at them with that remark about turning the place into a disco and calling it 'Pissoir'.

Such presence of mind goes beyond repartee. Aware, somehow, of all the options in a given situation, warily hatching out all possible contingencies, as Pfrumpy observed, incidentally wanting to know from us just what in any case made the difference between a basilica and a pissoir, Frank of no fixed address or employment, no known antecedents at all, lived restlessly in what might be described as a state of perpetual readiness.

Readiness, all right — but of a basilica turning into a pissoir, and then into a disco of that name?

Perhaps it could not be expected of a person continually hatching out all possible contingencies that he favoured any particular one of them. He needed to be put on track. With Frank, despite his energy and constant action, there was an absence of personal volition, almost a kind of autism, which his friends found disturbing. This in turn may have had to do with an ambiguous sexual aura about Frank that appealed to some, both men and women, but which others found eerie.

His girlfriend, Karen, with whom Frank shared an apartment during his first months in Berlin, said that whenever Frank went out of the house, or even just out of the room, she didn't know whether she was ever going to see him again. Karen couldn't stand the suspense and left him rather suddenly.[4]

Considering Frank's state of readiness in the Mercedes as it drove back from Potsdam to Berlin via Glienicker Bridge, for example, one cannot escape the question: readiness for what?

And what if he had been asleep in the car?

Pissoir had formerly been connected to Potsdamer Platz by a twin flight of stairs and to a subway station of that name by a tunnel. When the Wall was built the subway station Potsdamer Platz on the border of East and West went out of use. The entrances with the stairs leading down from the square were sealed.

Bulldozers and cranes had to be brought in to open the entrances and clear the rubble. Since for the time being nobody regarded Potsdamer Platz as falling within their jurisdiction, providing access to the buried disco had to be taken in hand, and incidentally paid for, by its trio of managers, Frank, Tom and Gerrit.

None of them had any money. Frank was living at the time on a student loan, Tom and Gerrit were broke. They were confident that their disco would make them a lot of money, which eventually it did, but none of the investors they approached for a loan shared that view.

It was three months before Frank raised enough money to hire the heavy machinery to excavate the stairs and give them access so that they could start refurbishing the place. Frank was cagey about where he had got the money from. The investor was rumoured to be an American multi-millionaire by the name of Frunton, Frutton or something.

The disco opened its doors to the public that summer. It was a gold mine. Until its forced closure three years later, Pissoir triumphed as the most popular disco in Berlin.

The tiled dome, the centrepiece of the Peacock Room, was left untouched. Frank and Gerrit heightened the brilliance of the mosaic by putting all the lighting in the conduit where patrons had once urinated, screening it off and letting the light flow up uniformly around the walls. The effect was stunning. The light was softened by filters that could change its colour and give it any texture from a smooth legato to a staccato pulse. The dome of the cavernous puddle was sealed with a Perspex cover. Light mushroomed out of it into the darkness above.

Seen at night across the wasteland of Potsdamer Platz, in a clearing fringed on one side by the looming shadow of the breached Wall and on the other by derelict buildings hemming in the dark, the shining perspex bubble looked to East Berliners like a spacecraft that had landed on the square.

It was a beacon visible far beyond Berlin. Kids arrived in their thousands, looking for adventure, breaching the porous Wall and flooding into the eastern part of the city. The former state to which all this had belonged was defunct, the new one not yet legitimised to take possession. Meanwhile the immigrants could do as they liked. The 20-something year-old cellar rats who swarmed underground through this no-man's-land, opening speakeasies in cellars and shopping malls in air-raid shafts, injected a flow of life into a city that had become a cemetery. It ran like an invisible flow of lava through the honeycomb of passageways beneath Berlin Mitte, pouring into the crannies and filling the holes until there was no place left for it to go. It erupted on the surface, a geyser with a burst of energy and a brightness which took the drowsy new immigrants to the upper world by surprise, because resurrection came upon the risen dead in the way that it always comes, suddenly and unexpectedly, quite differently from anything they could have dreamed even in a thousand-year sleep.

CHAPTER
3

Call me an observer.

It was in my capacity as an observer that I was present at the Institute for Experimental Physics in East Berlin on the occasion when Frank and I first met.

After a year of undergraduate physics, I had transferred to the school of moral philosophy, which in those days was a department of Marxism-Leninism, before moving back to the Institute to continue my postgraduate research into a phenomenon known as *entanglement*[5]. The concept originated as a feature peculiar to quantum physics. I felt it had a wider application worth investigating, and my research supervisor agreed. I was not among the experimenters at the Institute. I am not a qualified physicist. Being just an observer, I did not do anything other than observe.

In the winter semester of 1989, the Institute was in the process of setting up a long-term series of experiments to test the validity of Bell's Theorem.[6] These experiments probed the philosophical core of quantum physics. The subject is of extraordinary interest, perhaps for no one more so than for the uninitiated, to whom it must come as entirely fresh, never less than astonishing. It is almost a course in miracles. Unfortunately, this capacity to astonish cannot be communicated to a lay public without first covering some groundwork in quantum physics. The ascent may not always be easy to negotiate, but it is worth making the attempt. Footholds to assist the reader on the way up are indicated in the main body of the text. Footnotes elaborating points of interest or tricky variants are optional extras for the more ambitious climber, which can be safely ignored by the general reader just rambling through these pages.

At our Institute in East Berlin, and apparently at many others as well, the entrance to the magic mountain of quantum physics was guarded by a dragon in the shape of Werner Heisenberg and his Uncertainty Principle. The mathematical formalism leading to the Uncertainty Principle had to be tamed for practical use before one was allowed in. Whether students able to do the math understood what they were doing was another matter.

In the view of Richard Feynman and others, a much better introduction to quantum physics was given by an experiment the English physicist Thomas Young first carried out in the early 19th century. It is known as the double-slit experiment. It may seem a humble little affair, compared with experimental physics nowadays. Two hundred years on, however, the conundrum it poses continues to exercise the best minds.

A beam of coherent light is shone onto a solid wall in which two slits have been cut to a width small in proportion to the wavelength of the light. A photographic plate records where the light falls as discrete particles onto the screen on the far side of the wall. The plate is brighter in the areas where more light has fallen. When the right slit is opened and the left slit closed, most light is naturally recorded in the area on the screen behind the right slit, and vice-versa. When both slits are open, it might be expected that the record on the screen would show a composite image of the two cases seen before − light corpuscles, in the language of Newton, projected through the two slits would be aligned with the slits as two bars of brightness on the screen behind.

What one actually sees on the screen, however, are many alternating bars of light and dark known as an interference pattern, a feature that can only be explained if light is thought of not as particles but as waves.

As the waves emerge from the two slits they overlap. Imagine for a moment that these are waves of water. If it is the crests of the waves that overlap, the height of the waves increases, and if it is the troughs of the waves that coincide, the depth increases. If a crest of one wave coincides with the trough of another, there is neither increase nor decrease, the one cancels the other and the wave is annulled. Substituting light for water, these cancelled waves are what shows up on the screen as the dark bars of the interference pattern. The light bars are the result of wave crest coinciding with crest, or trough with trough (the water analogy illustrates the principle but is valid only up to a point). Young concluded that light was wavelike, contradicting Newton's view of it as being made up of particles.

The double-slit experiment has been repeated countless times in an attempt to resolve this contradiction. A version of it employing the electron gun of a TV set rather than a beam of coherent light was described by J. S. Bell in an elegantly written and very lucid little book of essays, *Speakable and Unspeakable in Quantum Mechanics*.[7]

Even when the electron barrage is reduced to the point where individual electrons are being fired at the screen one at a time with long intervals between, the telltale interference pattern of a wave still shows up. One just has to wait long enough for a sufficient number of electrons to pass through the slits and be recorded by a single dot as they hit the screen, where they then produce the characteristic interference pattern of a wave. The photographic plate shows not only areas that were dark when one slit was open and are bright when two slits were open, as might be expected, but also, inexplicably, areas that were bright with one slit open and now, with two slits open, are dark. Despite a general increase of electrons reaching the photographic plate, there has been a *decrease* in the brightness in some areas of the screen. This is the effect of wave crests (or troughs) coinciding and cancelling each other out. Areas on the screen that *are* hit by individual electrons when only one slit is open are somehow *not* hit when both slits are open.

Bell comments: 'Although each electron passes through one hole or the other (or so we tend to think) *it is as if the mere possibility of passing through the other hole influences its motion and prevents it going in certain directions*.[8] Here is the first hint of some queerness in the relation between possibility and actuality in quantum phenomena.'[9]

CHAPTER
3.1

Either/Or. Either corpuscles (Newton), or waves (Huygens). For centuries the debate of classical physics about the nature of light continued to divide opinion. Either/Or expresses an analytical view of the world, logic, taxonomy, order achieved on the basis of a fundamental division of things – a view by exclusion rather than inclusion, with a resulting tendency to find, unsurprisingly, contrariness in what is viewed. Intuitively, in the pairing Both/And, one senses an unbroken, seamless, inclusive view of the world.

The younger physicists of Heisenberg's generation seem to have dealt with the transition from *Either/Or* to *Both/And*, urged on them by the contrary nature in the inner workings of quantum phenomena[10], more easily than their older colleagues.

Wolfgang Pauli, Heisenberg's friend since their student days at Munich University, recognised in the *apparent dilemma* between wave and particle a principle of a universal nature, which allowed a 'contradiction-free description of all related phenomena, culminating in the establishment of the so called Uncertainty Principle.'[11] By 1925, the not much older De Broglie had already proposed that the dual description of light as both particle and wave might equally be applied to matter.

A generation later, Richard Feynman developed an already existing idea that particles hitherto assumed to pass through either the right slit or the left slit might actually pass through *both* slits; more, said Feynman, they might travel every possible trajectory simultaneously. Recent observation of particles that can apparently be in two places at once would seem to endorse the feasibility of Feynman's suggestion.

The problems that arise here with 'simultaneously' and 'in two places at once' are problems rooted in the *Either/Or*. Given the *Both/And* nature of the new spacetime of relativity as developed by Einstein, allowing different observers to come to different but equally valid conclusions about the time frame of the same events, Feynman's discovery that the spacetime description of a positron moving *forward* in time was exactly equivalent to the mathematical description of an electron (the anti-particle of a positron, same mass but opposite charge) moving *backward* through time along the same track, may strike one as a less fantastic consequence of the new physics than at first sight appears.

That light seemed to have both wave-like and particle-like properties remained mysterious even for the founders of quantum theory. The theory began with Max Planck's conjectures about the puzzle of black-body radiation, presented in Berlin in 1900, the year the Peacock Room opened for business beneath Potsdamer Platz.

The puzzle of black body radiation forced Planck to give up the classical assumption that the exchange of energy carried out in nature was a continuous, uninterrupted process. Reluctantly, under the pressure of the evidence, he guessed instead that the collections of vibrating atoms he called oscillators could receive or emit only discrete, quantized lumps of energy. Energy (E) could be emitted or absorbed only as quanta in multiples of an elementary quantity $\mathbf{E} = \mathbf{h} \times f$ (f is the frequency of vibration). The universal constant $\mathbf{h}$ representing the quantum of action is known as Planck's constant. The energy of the field passed through these discrete Planckian steps, but the size of the steps was so small that the discrete jumps from one energy level to another appeared to an observer to be a smooth flow.

Planck's notion of energy being given and taken as integral multiples of a fixed quantum of action x frequency, only in lump sums, so to speak, found its way into Einstein's new description of light. He concluded that the energy of light was not distributed evenly over the field, as classical physics supposed, but was concentrated in small, discrete bundles of light quanta, to be called photons. Niels Bohr used similar ideas in his theory of atomic structure[12] to explain the line spectra that had originally puzzled Planck. He assumed that the atomic system emitting the radiation could exist only in discrete energy states called eigenstates, and that states intermediate between such eigenstates were impossible.

Why should these quantum leaps from one eigenstate to another cause such consternation?

The word *unstet*, – unpredictable, capricious, fickle, all these nuances contribute to the flavour of a word frequently used by the older-generation founders of quantum theory – suggested the aesthetic dissatisfaction that must have been felt by physicists who had grown up with the predictable clockwork universe of Newtonian mechanics.[13] Once it had been detected, the Planck constant began cropping up all over the place, as unavoidable a universal constant as the speed of light.

But why? Why were there these eigenstates with nothing in-between, no way of telling when or how quantum leaps took place? What was going on in that in-between when the core matter of the universe missed a heartbeat and could not be accounted for? Did the universe momentarily go missing with it?[14]

Conceiving the decay of an atom from a higher energy state to a lower one to be a process comparable to radioactive decay, Einstein used statistical techniques, developed by Boltzmann (and also used by Planck) for dealing with the behaviour of collections of atoms. The probabilistic 'actuarial tables' of relativity helped him come to grips with the leaps of individual atoms from one energy state to another. He worked out the likelihood of such leaps taking place. He believed that later research would also determine why they took place when they did, but no such explanation predicting the unpredictable was ever forthcoming[15].

It seemed the quantum transitions were stochastic occurrences, occurring at random on a statistical basis. Chance, uncertainty, unpredictability, probabilities derived from statistical averages rather than the observed behaviour of individual constituents of matter, all such elements of 'fickleness' had to be incorporated at a fundamental level into a new description of the predictable universe which quantum physicists had inherited from Newton.

Everything in this universe, including the fabric of spacetime, was subject to quantum fluctuations that became increasingly turbulent when probed at increasingly small distances. Heisenberg's Uncertainty Principle ensured that nothing in it would ever be at rest. All things manifested quantum jitter, for if they did not one would know precisely where they were and with what momentum they were moving. This, however, the Uncertainty Principle had demonstrated to be impossible. You could know either the one or the other but not both at the same time. On a microscopic, sub-Planckian scale of distances, the quantum perturbations or undulations, the vibrating loops of modern string theory which were the successors to Planck's oscillators and Bohr's excited atoms, became so violent that they destroyed the notion of smoothly curving geometrical space required by Einstein to describe the macroscopic world. Quantum mechanics remained irreconcilable with General Relativity, let alone with what we prized as our common sense.[16]

CHAPTER
4

While shaving before lunch on Sunday as I listened to the twelve o'clock news on Radio SFB I heard there had been an accident on Glienicker Bridge in the early hours of the morning. A car had been recovered from the bed of the river. The three people inside it were dead. The police were still checking their identities. What had caused the car to plunge off the bridge was not yet known. The bridge had been closed while the car was being recovered but it was now open again for single-lane traffic.

My heart froze. My hand was shaking. Until I saw blood pouring down my cheek I didn't realise how badly I had cut myself. I sat down, drank a brandy and lit a cigarette. It took me quite some time to get over the initial shock, although the news had not taken me entirely by surprise.

Eventually I called the police to find out if the inmates of the car had been identified. If they were the people I suspected they were, I was a close friend, and might be able to help the police with their inquiries. I had driven with them to Potsdam in the same car, if it was the car, a black 6-litre Mercedes limousine, only the previous afternoon.

My call was put through to an officer who was working on the case. The car was indeed the car I had just described. Two of the passengers had been identified, a man and his wife, both of them Canadian citizens. Before the officer could go on I gave him their names myself. Somehow it was less unbearable than to have to listen to a stranger telling me the names of my dead friends down the telephone. Correct, he said.

And Frank, I asked? Who was Frank, the officer asked. The third victim, maybe, I said. Had he been identified too? If it was Frank I would be able to identify him. The officer said there had been no identification of the third victim as yet and asked if I would be willing to come round for that purpose.

A car was sent to pick me up and take me to the morgue.

Before the sheet covering the body lying in the morgue was drawn back for me to see the face, I *expected* it would be Frank's, but I was aware of the two quite opposite feelings within me about whose face I *wanted* to see on the slab.

How two such contradictory feelings can be in possession of a person, simultaneously and with equal intensity, was something I now experienced to such an extreme degree for the first time. For myself I felt intensely, selfishly and somehow trivially, the wish that it would not be Frank's face, the face of my friend dead, that I was about to see. I had an equally intense wish, on Frank's behalf but also partly on mine, not at all selfishly or trivially, that it would be Frank lying there after all, to see with my own eyes the proof that Frank was dead. Anything else would have been unforgivable. For the three years I had known him, Frank had seemed such an inseparable part of the troika he made up with Pfrumpy and Wilma in life that it seemed natural, more, it seemed *absolutely necessary*, that they would remain inseparable in death too. Frank had no alternative but to be dead. Anything else would have been a betrayal.

CHAPTER
5

The deeper that quantum theory probed the foundations of matter, the stranger the conclusions to which the theory led. The experiments carried out by Aspect *et al* during the early 1980s formed a link in a long chain of developments to the theory that had originated from Planck's quantum of action. Aspect conceived his famous experiment on the basis of Bell's Theorem[17], published twenty years previously by the physicist after whom it was named. Bell in turn had based his theory on a Bohm-Aharanov variant of a thought experiment put forward by Einstein, Podolsky and Rosen (known by the abbreviation EPR) thirty years before that, which in turn was a riposte to the Bohr-Heisenberg speculations of the previous decade concerning a reality dependent on an observer, the random nature of events that were mysteriously linked in the universe, and the inherent limitations imposed on our knowledge of it.

Einstein's position was that a particle must have a *separate reality independent of measurement*. It had momentum, position, a property called spin [18], and so on, even when such properties were not being measured. According to the EPR definition of 'reality', measurements carried out on one part of a system could not simultaneously affect the other part of the system. This principle of locality, as it is called, is an inviolable condition determined by the speed of light.

In a simplified version of an EPR-type experiment, one might envisage two entangled spin-1/2 particles with a total spin of O. The particles are separated and sent on different paths. Measurement of spin components can be made at will along the axes x, y and z. If, along the z-axis of Atom I, one measures a value of 'up' (+I), then the value along the z-axis of Atom 2 must necessarily be 'down' (-I).

According to EPR, the z-component of the spin of Atom 2 is an element of reality, since the measured value can be predicted with certainty without interference to Atom 2. The measurement of Atom I cannot have caused an interference with Atom 2, because in accordance with the criterion of locality arising from the theory of relativity, an interference cannot be propagated faster than the speed of light, i.e. some time, however small, must elapse between the two measurements. The result of the measurement, however, has already been determined *at the same moment* as the measurement undertaken on Atom I. But as one might equally well have measured the y-component of Atom I, the y-component of the spin of Atom 2 is no less an element of reality, as EPR sees it, than the actually measured z-component – and this contradicts the Uncertainty Principle, which states that only one spin component of an atom can have a value measurable with certainty.

To emphasise once again this important objection raised by EPR: it was not possible for a measurement on the first atom to determine the state in which the second atom found itself. To do so would entail some means of transmission operating beyond the speed of light, violating the definitive condition of reality known as locality. Such an operation was described by Einstein as 'spooky action at a distance', taking place outside the light cone – and that seemed to be out of the question.

The correct view according to Einstein, Podolsky and Rosen must be that the second atom had pre-prepared 'real' values for all properties corresponding to the measurements done on the first atom. Properties such as the spin of Atom 2 were determined prior to the measurement of Atom I. They must be dependent on some undiscovered quantities, so called *hidden variables* as yet to be described by quantum theory, not on measurements taken after the particles had separated. The EPR conclusion was therefore that quantum theory must be an incomplete description of reality in need of further revision.

The so called Copenhagen Interpretation (CI) of Bohr, Heisenberg and other younger-generation quantum physicists rejected the EPR premise of a reality independent of measurement[19]. Perhaps Bohr did not so much refute the EPR position as reaffirm his own. In his reply to the EPR thesis, Bohr reiterated that the two particles postulated in the thought experiment formed an irreducible quantum system, a so-called *entangled* state. Although, Bohr conceded, no direct signal could travel between the two photons making up the system (for that would indeed mean violating the condition of locality implied by Special Relativity and its universal constant, the speed of light), it nonetheless remained a fact that measurements made on one of them would influence the other. If a spin 'up' was measured for Atom 1 the corresponding spin for Atom 2 must be 'down', whatever the distance between them. Somehow it *knew* in what state it should find itself the instant a measurement was made on its twin particle, even if they were at opposite ends of the universe.

CHAPTER
5.1

Leaving aside the question of *hidden variables*, an impartial observer first had to consider the question of *hidden agendas*, for example of Professor Suckfüll.

The experiment at the Institute had been conceived under the aegis of its director Prof. Suckfüll eighteen months before the Wall came down. In the former German Democratic Republic one didn't become a director of anything, not even a kindergarten, without party approval, and party approval was given not necessarily to good physicists or kindergarten managers but to reliable, i.e. pliable exponents of Marxism-Leninism. Suckfüll, for reasons that need not be gone into here, *wanted* a result from the entangled particles experiment that was not in violation of the Inequality of Bell's Theorem[20], thus seeming to prove that the Copenhagen Interpretation was wrong and the EPR position right.

Suffice it to say that ideas of 'spooky action at a distance' did not go down well with the advocates of a materialist philosophy like Marxism[21], not with party bosses and therefore not with people dependent on their patronage in order to advance their careers. Thus Sichrovsky, the better physicist but the poorer diplomat, was passed over as director of the Institute in Suckfüll's favour and had to content himself with the position of vice-director. In this regard, there is no difference between careers in science and careers in any other field, except perhaps that the bias of the scientist is better concealed, from the layman at least.

Immediately after the Wall came down, Suckfüll was apparently taken ill and had not been seen at the Institute since. Jokes duly did the rounds regarding the degree of Suckfüll's *entanglement* with the State Security, how the one had gone AWOL and the other into immediate self-dissolution. After a decade of enforced self-effacement, Sichrovsky stepped into Suckfüll's place.

Appraising Suckfüll's successor, an impartial observer would be bound to look for *his* hidden agenda, too.

It would have been extraordinary had Sichrovsky shared his predecessor's distaste for Bohr's 'mysticism'[22] and for an interpretation of EPR that suspended laws of cause and effect not unimportant within a Marxist-Leninist scheme of things. Whatever the scientific merits of the case, Sichrovsky would have been *bound* to take the opposite view. He hated Suckfüll and all he stood for. It is inconceivable that such deep emotional involvement should not have affected his rational judgement. Scientists remain subject to the same passions as the rest of humanity and can do as little about them, probably less, as anyone else.

Sichrovsky naturally rejected the EPR position and supported Bohr's Copenhagen Interpretation. He did so before a shred of evidence had been gleaned from the experiment it had now become his task to supervise.

CHAPTER
5.2

There was no longer anything to hide, so the door to Sichrovsky's room, like the Wall, stood demonstratively open. This was a sign of the times – *glasnost*, accountability, democracy, access for all. Frank didn't even need to knock. He could just walk in, and he did, trailing a scarf that reached almost to the floor. At any other time there would have been more or less violent objections to such behaviour. Now it elicited no more than a gently querying 'Yes?' from the acting director of the Institute.

– Professor Sichrovsky? I have heard of the *most interesting* experiment your institute is planning. As a young engineering student, I played a modest, a really very *humble* part in the Orsay experiments of Alain Aspect, on which I gather your own investigation of Bell's Inequalities will be based. Aspect's conclusions were widely regarded at the time as confirmation of nonlocality in quantum mechanics. *However*, a few years after Aspect did his experiment *Franson* published a paper, as you know, arguing that the timing constraints in the Orsay experiments were *not* sufficient to confirm that the principle of locality was violated. The *crucial* time delay, of course, occurs between when a polarizer angle is changed and when this affects the statistics of detecting photon pairs. Well, I have been giving this problem some thought and have a few suggestions to make . . . .

The six of us sat in Sichrovsky's office and listened with some astonishment to a tall blonde young stranger standing not at all on ceremony in the doorway.

With one hand in his pocket he proceeded to deliver a long, fluent, emphatic and highly technical harangue on optical switches, polarizers and time-interval analysers, which for me at least was incomprehensible. From time to time he pulled at his scarf and gave his long mane of hair a vigorous shake, as if it interfered with what he was saying and needed to be got out of the way – a chronic nervous tic of Frank's that somehow came across as not in the least nervous but just the reverse, completely confident, as if he were quite used to shaking off a never ending succession of these invisible pursuers and in fact rather enjoyed it.

Had Frank looked round the door and inquired after Professor Suckfüll – and it was perhaps surprising he didn't, the name plate identifying Suckfüll as the inmate was still in place, after all – the effect of his entrance would have been ruined despite this display of brilliance. But Frank's performance was word-perfect. He delivered exactly what the people meeting in Sichrovsky's office wanted at that moment.

Frank had a knack of delivering what people wanted, as I would discover, in all sorts of circumstances, and it enabled him to get away with things they wouldn't have allowed anyone else. They didn't mind him barging in, who the hell he was or where he came from or that he had neglected to tell them his name.

– Well now, that's not uninteresting . . . by no means . . . *hmmm!* . . . but let's, er, *seeee*, shall we?

Sichrovsky got up and pulled down a wall chart showing the technical installations of the experimental set-up. His assistant Jens got up with him, Frank moved forward from the doorway where he had remained standing throughout his address, the two graduate students followed, everyone but Peter and I soon crowded round eagerly.

Peter, being something of a geek, like many mathematicians, probably had a fair idea of what all the technical talk was about, but if he did so he wasn't letting on. With Peter one could not be sure if his diffident manner was due to shyness, or modesty, or the arrogance of the caste of mathematicians, among whom Peter ranked as a medium-high to high priest. Sallow, bespectacled, unshaven, carrying with the utmost care – indeed, almost as if having to balance it – the lofty bald dome of his head so that the fragile filaments of the brain enmeshed there would not be disturbed, Peter looked geeky mathematician as

Chopin looked romantic composer or Savonarola looked zealot priest.

– We had to face problems of drifts.

– Hmmm.

– Making it necessary to average out . . .

– Yes. And another problem: the commutation by the switches was incomplete, because the incidence angle was not exactly the Bragg angle for all rays . . .

– Ah!

Why Peter had got involved in Suckfüll's project was unclear. He was billed as Suckfüll's mathematical adviser. But statistics, the sort of applied mathematics required here, were not Peter's thing at all.

The meeting dragged on. We both got bored and went out into the corridor for a smoke. Peter's slow, elaborate way of smoking, involving long, secretive ingestions of smoke and little puffs of exhalation, delivered as casual asides, evoked an enjoyment of Turkish water-pipe rituals rather than the consumption of Intershop cigarettes. You peered at this Oriental Peter through the smoke and wondered what he was thinking about.

CHAPTER
5.3

There was in fact a great deal to hide, now more than ever. All your entrances and your exits, your phone calls, your friends, how you spent your evenings, your drinking habits, your taste in music, your taste in people, relatives in the West who sent you parcels, all this had been subject to scrutiny and might be held against you. Whose side had you been on? If you had been on the right side then you were on the wrong side now, and vice versa. Somewhere it was all on file, down to your last laundry bill.

How omnipresent the State Security had been mattered less than how omnipresent people feared they had been. This magnifying effect has always been the key to the success of all state security systems.

The first figures to be leaked out of the secret archives now under the guard of citizens' committees suggested that anything from five to fifteen percent of the population, or between one and two million people, had worked for the State Security as informers against their fellow citizens. The figures were outwardly dismissed as wildly exaggerated. But the private reaction of many people had been: what, *only*?

Somewhere it was all on file, who, when, where, what, and in connection with whom. It was rumoured that the files would soon be made public. Soon there would be a reckoning.

Regarding security systems: more effective (and cheaper) than surveillance by an omniscient state security is the principle of mutual mistrust among the people. Mistrust is a natural collaborator of envy, and there is envy everywhere, in great quantities. The nurturing of undesirable human qualities is the hallmark of all dictatorships. In the long run their cynicism is far more dangerous than their secret police.

Individuals like Suckfüll, who had openly benefited from the old system, moved out of the line of fire to their well-provisioned dachas in the country. Others, like Sichrovsky, who had openly suffered setbacks under the old regime, now carried their heads high. Among those now carrying their heads high were Peter and Ulla.

I lived in a garret above the apartment where Peter and Ulla were domiciled with their two children. Had I been an Informer in addition to being an Observer, it would have been easy for me to report whatever went on in their household by watching what went on in their kitchen through the hole in my bedroom floor. But I wouldn't have needed to go to that trouble. Many evenings I spent in that kitchen myself.

Ulla and Peter were Church people. Church didn't mean religion so much as political opposition. Quite certainly down on Ulla's and Peter's files would have been the fact that they had not sent their children to a state kindergarten but to a private kindergarten run by the Church, a doubtful privilege for which they had even been prepared to pay money.

On Luther's home turf there was a certain tradition of Church issues being used as a stalking-horse to shoot all sorts of projectiles at the enemy lines. It wasn't exactly tolerated by State Security, nor was it stamped out brutally under their heel. Heretics were kept under observation. They were bad boys, but they were our own.

When the Wall came down and people looked from outside into our dark little box of a country something quite unexpected was noticed.

Despite everything there had been, as the inmates rather awkwardly admitted, a sort of snugness to the place. If you stayed in the box (millions had left it) it was because you had come to terms with it and settled down in the undemanding, cosy atmosphere of a state-planned collective, a nice warm brew of mediocrity where everyone was on an equal footing. Health, housing, jobs, education, the price of beer and pork chops – the basics of life were guaranteed. There was no elbowing aside, because there was nowhere to get ahead. No one earned more than twice or at most three times what their neighbour earned.

And on the down side? You did not look at the Wall. You kept away from border areas altogether. You avoided reminding yourself unnecessarily of the cost of the compromise you had made. But to the great majority of those who remained in the box, it can truthfully be said, security mattered more than freedom. Within the always elastic scope of the Marxist dialectic, a case might quite easily be made for the contention that there is indeed no greater security than imprisonment.

There might be mutual mistrust towards neighbours as potential informers. But mistrust had also fostered, had it not, a fellowship of Us against Them, claimed intimacy in a common cause, the cosy atmosphere of kitchen conspiracies such as the one to which I belonged with Ulla and Peter.

Where is my friend without my enemy?

The symmetry between matter and antimatter, as Dirac showed, implies that for every particle there exists an antiparticle with equal mass and opposite charge.

Opposites are arbitrary points along a line in the same human plane. It binds profligacy and generosity, timidity and prudence, love and hate into one skein. Here, along this line connecting opposites, is where we have our being, like particles in always alternating states of repulsion and attraction. Mistrust may tone up and by degrees mellow into friendship, cosiness shade down into the too narrow confinement of a prison cell. They are extensions, or to borrow a word from quantum mechanics, entanglements of the same thing.

Take Feynman's discovery that the spacetime description of a positron moving forward in time is exactly equivalent to the mathematical description of its anti-particle, the electron, moving backward through time along the same track.

Between quantum leaps (rising up from or falling back down) particles tend to return to their original eigenstates, and these are the states of minimum energy. Here they are at rest in their native state, one might say: at home: but how could this be without unrest in changing to and from those other states by which such notions as home and rest would have to be defined?

Certain analogies to the inner workings of human situations can be derived from quantum mechanics, be they no more than metaphors, figures of speech.

CHAPTER
5.4

About a year and a half before the fall of the Wall Ulla was arrested, charged with subversive activities jeopardising the national interest and detained by the State Security. She was not sent to prison, however, not even put on trial. Within days of her arrest Ulla was taken to the border and dumped on the other side, *shoved off*, in the jargon current at the time, to the West.

Peter tried to manage on his own for a while, but failed. He had a nervous breakdown. Ulla's elder sister Petra arrived from the country, another red-cheeked APC[23] girl like Ulla, just bigger and heartier, to keep house and look after the two little girls she had left behind.

The box in which we lived had antennae on the roof that made it possible for our TV sets to receive broadcasts from the West. We knew that something was afoot. Inside our box, where we were never told anything but lies, one sensed the scurrying of rats behind the wainscoting, the activities of greedy rat-like persons driven by their survival instinct, peering anxiously out of their holes, gathering and hiding their hoard under the floorboards. Mitigating circumstances, though not an outright amnesty at this late stage of the game, might still be negotiated by dumping political dissidents over the border rather than dumping them in prison. For, of course, now the Wall was down there would be a purge, or a reckoning at least, and those on our side of it who had been responsible for the dumping would be asked to pay. That was how we explained the lenience shown to Ulla at the time.

The day after the Wall was breached Ulla came home. Ulla wept, Peter wept, the twins cried and laughed for joy to see the family reunited.

An uneasy euphoria, pitched between laughter and tears, relief and anger, expectation and disappointment, took possession of the country.

Brought up on mistrust, we were wary of the newcomers who came over from the West, squatting in derelict houses, running businesses out of vacant premises along the death zone, as if they were playing a game. We were their poor relations, irritated to see them having fun and envious of their success. We kept them at arm's length. We knew our place, and it was one in which the plumbing didn't work, or there was no plumbing at all, but which for all that was morally superior, in principle if not always in practice.

Sometimes we felt quite bitter in our moral superiority. In winter I had to fetch coal from the basement and carry it in a scuttle up five flights of stairs to heat my room in the attic. When the Wall came down some of us had treated ourselves to a night in a West Berlin hotel and discovered we needed to be shown by the staff how the bathroom appliances worked, a humiliation so deep that it had ruined our stay. So it was surprising how easily Frank moved in under our defences and won our confidence.

Sichrovsky invited him to join the project team. Frank's enthusiasm was infectious. For the first few months, at least, we saw him at the Institute almost every day. We had lunch together in the canteen. In the evenings he came back with Peter and me and was adopted as a member of the kitchen cabinet. He did card tricks and told funny stories, twitching his long mane of hair, shaking off the invisible pursuers. He had no airs. He was entirely natural. We laughed a lot when Frank was around. He became a great favourite with Ulla and the twins.

– With Frank everything's such fun, as if all life were just a game.

Ulla made this remark within Peter's hearing, so it could have been intended not just as praise of Frank but as criticism of Peter. With Peter nothing much was fun, life was not a game, and no amount of nervous breakdown during her absence could account for Ulla's impression that Peter had seemed more upset by her deportation than overjoyed at her return. In bed he did not touch her. He turned his face to the wall and pretended to sleep.

Ulla suspected that during her absence Peter had been having an affair with her sister Petra, and now that Petra was gone he was depressed because he missed her. She confided in me, which may have been her way of getting me to tell her if I had seen or heard anything that would confirm her suspicions. I put her mind at rest. Ulla would have liked to confront Peter, was certainly not afraid to, but, as she remarked to me, she felt it beneath her dignity to do so.

On his visits to the house Frank started bringing with him a Canadian woman he had first introduced to me in connection with the thesis I was writing at the time. She had travelled all over the world in the course of her work as a press photographer, from the jungles of Sumatra to the Himalayas. Now she wanted to do a photo project about our house in Berlin Mitte, the building, the inmates, the neighbourhood they lived in – people who until the Wall came down had seldom eaten a banana, never seen a mango or a papaya, let alone the Himalayas.

We felt flattered but were at the same time incredulous that a photographer who had seen and done all the things that Wilma had done could be in the least bit interested in our drab little community. We were amazed to see a woman wearing a chequered headgear like Yasser Arafat's get down on her knees to take a picture of a grimy passageway or in order to photograph the dilapidated staircase from a particular angle. She ferreted around in the cellar, putting up lights to take pictures of me filling my coal scuttle. She took pictures of the twins playing hopscotch with the other children in the neighbourhood. She took pictures of Peter and Ulla sitting side by side on the stairs of the front porch.

Although Wilma knew nothing about the personal history of Peter and Ulla she saw their unhappiness in the photos she took of them. She saw something we didn't see. Within the same place they sat together as if they were in different zones, she said, *next to each other but not together*, as if they were on either side of the 'invisible wall' that divided them.

At the time when Wilma first looked at the photos with me and Frank, and described to us what she could see in them, she didn't know anything about Ulla's deportation and exile, separated from Peter for eighteen months on the other side of the Wall. What Frank had told me about Pfrumpy's wife was true. Wilma possessed something like second sight. Wilma was a psychic.

CHAPTER
6

Within a couple of years during the mid-1920s, Heisenberg and Schrödinger, using different approaches that in the end turned out to be mathematically equivalent, succeeded in giving formal expression to the probability wave concept. Schrödinger's Equation, being the more easily applicable of the two, is to this day used regularly in calculations of wave mechanics.

In classical mechanics, electrons had been conceived as point particles pursuing definite trajectories calculable from the equations of the particle's initial position and momentum. In his first interpretation of wave mechanics, Schrödinger thought the electron was spread out in space and had a density given by the square of the amplitude (height) of the wave. He assumed the waves to be 'smeared-out' electrons, representing – or being, this was not quite clear, one of those crucial points slurred over by even the greatest physicists – actual stuff, matter. Though not concentrated at a particular point as in classical mechanics, in Schrödinger's view the intensity of the wave in space did represent some actual 'quantity' of the electron, spread or smeared out, which was to be found there.

Problems arose with Schrödinger's interpretation of electron waves. It failed to explain why, when a particle was detected, it always had a well-defined position in space rather than the wavelike characteristic, as projected by Schrödinger, of being spread out in space.

Max Born modified Schrödinger's material wave interpretation in terms of probability.

Places at which the square of the absolute value of the amplitude of the wave was large would be places where the electron was more likely to be found, and in places where the square of the absolute value of the amplitude was small the electron was less likely to be found. What Schrödinger had interpreted as the *density of the electron* to be found at some point, Born radically reinterpreted as the *density of the probability of finding the electron* there.

The classical concept, in fact a metaphor, of the electron as a point particle moving on a well-defined path around the nucleus of the atom thus came to be replaced in wave mechanics by another metaphor, clouds representing the probable location of electrons. In quantum mechanics, one could speak only of approximate trajectories. Only the average of all the electrons in the cloud was significant, but because the number of electrons might be very large (in a cloud of hydrogen atoms, by contrast, there would be only a single electron) their average properties derived from their average distribution could be taken as a close approximation to their actual behaviour.

Heisenberg refined Born's position as to the nature of particle waves with reference to electromagnetic waves. They 'were taken to be not real waves but probability waves. Their intensity at any point determines the probability of a quantum of light being absorbed or emitted by an atom at this place . . . thus a completely new concept was incorporated into theoretical physics. What the probability wave signified was a sort of tendency towards certain events. It introduced a strange kind of physical reality, lying somewhere between possibility and actuality.'[24]

Late in life Heisenberg refined that position further.

'The laws of nature which we formulate mathematically in quantum theory deal no longer with the particles themselves but with our knowledge of them.'

And finally:

'The concept of objective reality . . . evaporated . . . into the mathematics that represents no longer the behaviour of elementary particles, but rather our knowledge of this behaviour.'[25]

Objective + reality + evaporated.

To those who still wondered what all the quantum physics fuss was about these three words of Heisenberg's delivered a punch of an answer, a technical knockout, staving the bottom out of the hoop-bound barrel of the world with which all of us felt comfortably familiar.

But how did objective reality evaporate?

Because some quantum physicists concluded that without the presence of an agent – it might be convenient to use the term observer – to perceive and/or measure the microscopic events described by them – those events did not take place.

During his conversation with Einstein in Berlin in the fall of 1926, Heisenberg was dumbfounded by Einstein's remark that you had to wait for the theory to find out what it was you were able to observe. ('Erst die Theorie entscheidet darüber, was man beobachten kann')[26]. This seemed to Heisenberg to be standing things on their head. Surely the time-honoured procedure in physics was to observe what happened and then describe it.

But what *was* it that one observed happening?

Heisenberg wrestled with this problem during the nights he worked on his discovery of the Uncertainty Principle.

'But what could be wrong here? The path of the electron in the cloud chamber[27] existed, one could observe it . . . the conversation I had with Einstein came into my mind and I remembered his remark: *Erst die Theorie entscheidet darüber, was man beobachten kann* . . . we had always just told ourselves that the path of the electron in the cloud chamber was something one could observe. But perhaps what one actually observed was rather less than that. Perhaps all one could perceive was just a discrete series of imprecisely determined locations of the electron. For one does in fact see just single drops of water in the chamber, which are certainly much more substantial than an electron . . .'[28]

The key words here, the point at which Heisenberg's great insight seems to have ignited, are 'imprecisely determined'. Until then, he seems to be saying, he had been confident that the water drops he was looking at in the cloud chamber showed the path of the electron. Now it struck him they might show *rather less* than that, features of an electron's path that in themselves were imprecisely determined, or vice versa, a quick calculation made on the assumption of such imprecision, a viable mathematical explanation incorporating some uncertainty factor[29], might retrospectively give support to the observation it *was* something imprecise that he had observed with his senses, not an electron's path, but what might be an electron's path, the possibility of an electron, the *imprecise being* of an electron.

Heisenberg's 'observation' of the events in the cloud chamber was something he had to *make up his mind he had seen*. Observation thus becomes inseparable from hypothesis, from a theory about what has been observed, just as Einstein had said (or as Heisenberg interpreted Einstein as having said).[30]

In the same conversation with Heisenberg, in a critical aside a propos the positivism of Ernst Mach, a physicist-philosopher who had exerted considerable influence on him as a young man, Einstein dropped an intriguing hint as to the difficulties encountered when attempting to define 'observation'.

'Mach acts as if we knew all right what the word 'observe' means; and it's because he thinks he can dodge the decision about 'objective or subjective' on this point that his concept of simplicity takes on such a suspiciously commercial character: economy of thought . . . the simplicity of natural laws is also an objective fact, and what we need is to establish the correct balance of the subjective and objective aspects of simplicity within a correct conceptual framework. But that's very difficult.'

How much have I seen?

More, or, like Heisenberg having to make up his mind about quite what he had seen in the cloud chamber, *rather less*?

How much of what I have seen was already out there, how much has been attributed to it by me?

Bohr addressed the problem, without managing to shed new light on it.

'An independent reality in the ordinary physical sense can neither be ascribed to the phenomena nor to the agencies of observation...the circumstance that in interpreting observations use has always to be made of theoretical notions entails that for every particular case it is *a question of convenience* [31] at which point the concept of observation involving the quantum postulate with its inherent 'irrationality' is brought in.'

The 'question of convenience' as to where the concept of observation should be brought in still bothered J.S.Bell forty years later.

'The subject-object distinction is indeed at the very root of the unease that many people still feel in connection with quantum mechanics. Some such distinction is dictated by the postulates of the theory, but exactly when or where to make it is not prescribed.'

And in another of his essays:

'The problem is this. Quantum mechanics is fundamentally about 'observations'. It necessarily divides the world into two parts. A part which is observed and a part which does the observing. The results depend in detail on just how this division is made, but no definite prescription for it is given. All that we have is a recipe which is sufficiently unambiguous for practical purposes.'[32]

Einstein's desire for a correct balance of the subjective and objective aspects, Bohr's question of convenience as to where the quantum postulate should be brought in, Bell's uncertainty about when or where the subject-object distinction should be made – all these reflections revolve around a concept that may be sufficiently unambiguous for practical purposes, but which otherwise remains very ambiguous indeed: the wave function.

CHAPTER
6.112

'Given any object, all the possible knowledge concerning that object can be given as its wave function. This is a mathematical concept the exact nature of which need not concern us here – it is composed of a (countable) infinity of numbers. It permits one to tell with what probabilities the object will make one or other impression on us if we let it interact with us. These interactions are also called observations, or measurements. The important point is that the impression which one gains at an interaction may modify the probabilities with which one gains the various probable impressions at later interactions, i.e. the impression, called also the result of an observation, modifies the wave function of the system.[33] The modified wave function is, furthermore, in general unpredictable before the impression gained at the interaction has entered our consciousness: it is the entering of an impression into our consciousness which alters the wave function because it modifies our appraisal of the probabilities for different impressions which we expect to receive in the future. At this point consciousness enters the theory unavoidably and unalterably.'[34]

CHAPTER
6.1121

'In quantum theory, one hardly sees any other possible issue than postulating that the stochastic (random) event, or quantal transition, or collapse of the wave function, is induced by an act of consciousness on the observer's part...in the Schrödinger cat paradox[35], the cat will be killed or left alive according to whether the decay electron of a radionuclide goes or does not go through a Geiger counter. In ordinary statistical mechanics the cat is already either dead (D state) or alive (L state) when the observer opens the box. In quantum mechanics it is believed that it is the awareness of the observer opening the box that collapses the wave function. Should we then say, according to the quantum mechanics rules, that after the atom had decayed but before the observer takes a look, the cat is in a superposition, or interference state *(i.e. in both D and L states)*[36], denoting the respective possibilities that the electron does or does not trigger the counter?'[37]

CHAPTER
6.1122

– All right?

I nodded to the white-smocked assistant in the morgue and she bent forward to fold down the cover over the figure lying on the slab. Until this moment there had been a dead man there whom nobody knew. It was my task to identify him – and for the first time I became aware of the enormity of my responsibility.

There might have been a strong probability it was Frank but we weren't certain. There was a small remaining probability that the man was not Frank and Frank was not dead. Until this moment, strictly speaking, Frank would not have been one hundred percent dead. If he had been, there would have been no need for the police to have brought me here. He still might have been lying unconscious on the bank of the Havel or sleeping the night off in the apartment of someone he had met at the wedding, or Frank in any number of possible states analogous to the hypothetical quantum-mechanical superposition 'neither dead nor alive'. It might be a complete stranger lying there on the slab, who had been with Wilma and Pfrumpy in the car recovered from the river.

Only after I had identified the man, said 'Yes, that's him', would Frank be registered in the police files as dead. Only then would Frank be officially dead. There would be no more 'would' about it. When I passed from the subjunctive mode into the indicative and said 'Yes, that's him', I would in a manner of speaking be collapsing the wave function, it would in the end be by my act of consciousness that Frank became irreversibly dead, or, if you will, that the dead person on the slab became irreversibly Frank.

CHAPTER
7

Within thirty-six hours of the police notifying the Canadian Embassy in Berlin of the deaths of two Canadian citizens, Lawrence Peabody had flown in from Montreal. Father and son Peabody had served father and son Pfrumpter as legal advisers for two generations. It was neither quite a personal relationship between the two families, nor quite a business one. It was a personalised business relationship. Peabody was a whirling midget of a man, affectionately known since childhood by the nickname Pea. That was what Pfrumpy had always called him, and Pfrumpy was what Pea had always called his client Mr Pfrumpter.

Babaji, called back from holiday in Switzerland, was so distraught that he was incapable of handling anything. It was I that went to the airport to meet Pea and bring him to the hotel I booked for him just round the corner from Pfrumpy's house off the Kurfürstendamm in West Berlin. It was I who gave Pea the first briefing on the accident that had happened on Glienicker Bridge.

Peabody's prompt arrival in Berlin was occasioned not so much by any suspicious circumstances of his client's death as by the size of the fortune Pfrumpy had left — something around a quarter of a billion dollars. There were odds and ends like life insurance claims for Pea to tie up. It was only when we got into the Mercedes 600 he had hired and I drove out with him to Glienicker Bridge that I began to appreciate how puzzling were the circumstances in which Pfrumpy had met his death.

Glienicker Bridge is a steel construction. There are steel girders standing upright, a row of irregular rectangles transected by diagonals that form two triangles between two uprights. As the uprights are set quite close together, it is unlikely that even a small car would have enough room to pass between them. The presence of the diagonal girder rules out this possibility altogether.

In the week before the accident, however, a municipal truck involved in work on the girders along one side of the bridge had crashed into them. The damage was serious enough to cause the removal of one upright and the two diagonal girders on either side of it. The girders were removed on a Friday and were due to be replaced by new ones the following Monday.

Over the weekend the gap left by the three girders that had been removed was closed off with a double line of red and white tape and flanked by Caution-Danger signs. In the meantime, further temporary measures had been taken to seal the gap that would now have to remain without the original girders for as long as the police investigations continued, but those were the only precautions which had been considered necessary at the time.

Behind the girders a very sturdy metal balustrade provides a second barrier between the road and the river. As we drove past we could clearly see the hole that had been torn in this balustrade when the car plunged off the bridge.

Peabody parked the car in a lay-by at the Potsdam end of the bridge. Then we walked back to the spot where the car had plunged into the river. Peabody took out a tape and measured the distance between the two girders left standing, the height of the kerb, the height of the fence and the width of the hole made in it by the car. Using a magnifying glass, he carried out a minute inspection of the two uprights on either side of the gap through which the car must have passed. He took Polaroid photos of the site.

We returned to the car, turned round and drove back as soon as there were no other cars on the bridge. As we came level with the gap in the girders Peabody glanced across, pulled hard on the wheel and swerved towards it.

— If you try to swing off at a right angle into this thing when you're going at a good lick you're going to have to brake, or you'll flip over.

Right? But when you brake you lose the momentum you're going to need to crash through that steel balustrade. Damned if I know how he did it. Do you?

But I was as baffled as he was.

The lawyer who behaved like a cop spent the afternoon examining the official police reports, the autopsy results, the forensic tests that had been carried out on the car, before giving the car a very thorough going over himself.

I accompanied Pea on a second visit to the bridge at three o'clock in the morning, the time the accident had happened. In the hour we spent there only five cars crossed the bridge. There was a fifteen-minute interval when no cars crossed at all. It was during this interval that Pea brought the Mercedes 600 round broadside, aligned it with the gap between the girders and drove right up to the barrier sealing the gap.

– Damned if I know how he did it, unless he did what I've just done. And even then he wouldn't have got through. Too slow. Well, say that's what happened . . .

We knew that Pfrumpy had been driving. His body was still stuck behind the steering wheel when the car was recovered from the river.

– In which case, it was a deliberate act. And even then . . .

But Pfrumpy had had two other people with him in the car, I said. According to the autopsy report, Frank had had quite a bit to drink, Wilma just a little, Pfrumpy none at all. Were we to imagine that both passengers had concurred when Pfrumpy stopped the car on the middle of the bridge, reversed it, aimed the car at the gap and drove through?

– Or were they perhaps both asleep?

– Perhaps.

Pea sounded very depressed. We drove for most of the way back to his hotel in baffled silence, and a few hours later he caught a plane back to Montreal.

The entrance to Pissoir was hung with the large black and white photos Wilma had made of its excavation and refurbishment. They were part of the series she later published as a book. The series was initiated by commissions Wilma received at the time from Canadian and American newspapers to capture the atmosphere of the city during the fall of the Wall and after. In a personal file, Wilma kept to herself the photographs that had inspired the series, her portraits of Frank.

Wilma's interest in Frank was the same interest that inspired all of her best portrait work. She thought Frank was beautiful and she wanted to capture that beauty and find out what it was.

The day she came across Frank, Tom and Gerrit excavating the puddle on Potsdamer Platz Wilma wrote in the notebook where she logged her photo shoots: 'Here is a man looking for something, but will he know when he has found it?' – which on the face of it was clairvoyant, as the picture under which she wrote these words showed three men looking down over the rim of the cavernous puddle. Inside the puddle they found what Frank believed for a while to have been a basilica before it finally turned out to have been a public convenience.

Wilma became interested in what she dubbed the 'basilica Frank', someone who occupied intermediate positions that turned out to be untenable in the long run.

Karen was one of these untenable positions. She moved out of the apartment she had been sharing with Frank. Unable to pay the rent on his own, Frank moved into Gerrit's tent on Potsdamer Platz and lived there with him and Tom for several months until Pissoir briefly made them rich. Wilma asked Karen why she had moved out on Frank, and made a note of her cryptic response under a snapshot of Karen glancing back over her shoulder as she walked off down the street.

'You know, a regular girl like me can't afford a luxury creature like Frank. The trouble with Frank is that he doesn't know what he wants, so how can he expect me to? I'm just a waitress, OK?'

Wilma did a second photo shoot with Basilica Frank at the former Palace of the Republic. Another white elephant of a building, another of those Communist eyesores. Like those endless monuments to Soviet Friendship, the Palace was a sort of arts-cum-community centre hogging a chunk of prime real estate by the river in East Berlin. Unloved, unfunded, and above all uninhabitable, according to a post-Wall Western expertise about the quantities of carcinogenic asbestos that had gone into its construction, the culture centre remained closed to the public, maybe for ever. The only centre it now served as was as the centre of an early marriage row between East and West about whether to demolish it and, if so, what should replace it.

Meanwhile the inventory was to be auctioned off. This included an organ in the main auditorium, pictures, lights, fixtures, carpets, wash basins, toilet bowls, office and cloakroom appliances, ten thousand auditorium seats without legs. Flush after the successful opening of Pissoir, enthralled by his new-found wealth, Frank went along to the auction with Wilma to bid for the bar.

The circular bar had a draped shell or mantle made of solid steel, with a surface consisting of thousands of steel rods arranged like organ pipes. It had been commissioned from a leading artist of the former Republic as a tribute to what used to be one of its foremost industries, its steel works. Casting the shell in solid steel was a masterpiece of technology. The cost was enormous. But they accomplished the task, delivering a solid-steel mantle for a bar weighing many tons.

This was the bar that until not long ago commanded the foyer outside the main auditorium of the Palace of the Republic, where the party held its plenary sessions, celebrated its rituals, its triumphs in honour of itself. Frank knew the man who used to operate the gigantic machinery, which could shift walls and floors in that auditorium to design a space of almost any shape or size. Tens of thousands of Marks had to be poured in daily just to keep the machinery in working order. Before he passed into history, the stage machinist of the Palace of the Republic gave Frank, Wilma and a select group of connoisseurs a demonstration of what he could do with his auditorium. The centrepiece of the Palace of the Republic was a hall which seated 10,000 people, and the machinist could stand in his control room flicking switches to design whatever space he wanted, causing the whole thing to rise, sink, pivot, tilt, expand or contract on half a million well-lubricated ball bearings.

Nobody wanted the bar. Frank bought the steelworkers' masterpiece at a knockdown price, a fraction of what it had cost to make it.

– What are you going to do with it, Frank?

– Put it in storage.

– And then?

– Open a bar?

Frank laughed.

– Actually, I was thinking of sending it on a world tour.

Wilma took a rich drag on her clove cigarette and handed it to Frank.

– Touring as what?

– Something theatrical. I don't know, there are still the details to be worked out.

Meanwhile the stripped-down skeleton of the bar, a naked round steel thing without its organ-pipe mantle, was installed for service in Pissoir. Only the mantle went into storage.

Wilma's perception of Frank while excavating the puddle on Potsdamer Platz was of someone looking for something who wouldn't recognise it when he found it. Maybe, as she acknowledged in the margin of her work book, she was really thinking of him finding Wilma.

During the months-long shooting of the Pissoir and Palace-of-the-Republic series she came to see the fault line in Frank's nature: the lack of a personal volition, of his wanting anything particular in life. He roamed around in his vagrant existence, a stray dog lifting his leg in basements and underground shafts, dirty and derelict places, busy with one thing and another, none of them indispensable to him, they could equally well have been something else. There was a lack of the act of consummation, taking up into his life all those things he had unearthed at the bottom of it, finding a place for them as part of a personal history, furnishings that documented Frank in tenure, in possession of his own life.

In Frank's obsession with opening up things that were closed, revitalising condemned houses and disused air raid shelters or digging things up out of the ground, Wilma could sense, beyond the curiosity, also the fear of what he might find. Frank's vitality fed off his preoccupation with death, his energy was galvanised by the prospect of its extinction. Whether this was the case or not, the fact that Wilma saw it as the case, and told Frank so, who would have been unable to see it for himself, irresistibly had its effect on him. Frank couldn't escape the emphatically personalising influence that characterised Wilma's relationships with people. She was unable to just let them be, she on one side, so to speak, they on the other. Frank couldn't escape being drawn by Wilma into that bonding place she always managed to create in between. She won his trust.

By bringing about in Frank an awareness of her perception of him, Wilma supplied him with a pattern he didn't have, put into his life, and perhaps also into his death, as I shall seek to show, something to replace the lack of Frank's own volition – and that was Wilma's own volition and awareness, how Wilma saw or rather surmised the world, divining something other behind the appearances of things.

Perhaps Frank's submission to Wilma was no more than an expression of the fact that she had already captured him in her pictures, put frames around his actions and sized him up before he had realised what was happening to him. She had acquired power over his image. Twenty-six levels below the surface of the earth in a disused boiler room under Tempelhof Airport, a wartime Nazi legacy that was the ground zero of Berlin, she persuaded Basilica Frank to pose naked for her against piles of corroded sheet metal, looking wide-eyed into the flash light, hands hovering by his thighs in another untenable position, ready to make good his shame and cover up from Wilma's eyes what her camera had already seen and recorded, a twenty-eight year-old man's penis and testicles arrested at the stage of development of a ten year-old child.

CHAPTER
8.1

Frank dreamed he had been buried alive and that Wilma, a homebound Eurydice in an unfamiliar role-reversal, brought him back above ground to the light of the upper world. He could hear rain, but with a sound different from the rain he heard on the tent. When he opened his eyes, for a moment he didn't know where he was. Then he saw through the window the leaves of the chestnut tree on which the rain was making a different sound, and remembered he was on the second floor of Pfrumpy's house. It was Babaji coming into the room with a cup of tea that had woken him. I dreamed I was buried alive and Wilma brought me back above ground, Frank said sleepily to Babaji, and sat up in bed to receive the tea[38].

She's very good at that sort of thing, said Babaji, adding as he placed the cup in Frank's hands: 'Darjeeling remains for me the best tea in the world.'

Babaji never omitted the loyal reference to Darjeeling when he brought house guests a cup of tea, as I found out myself when I was honoured with one. Babaji sometimes brought tea to house guests, as a favour and purely on impulse. The old gentleman was in no sense a retainer or house servant from whom one could have requested such a service unless he volunteered it.

Babaji was working for an insurance company in Darjeeling when contacted by Peabody in 1970. On the death of Pfrumpter Senior, CEO of Pfrumpter Pharmaceuticals, Peabody had been dispatched to India to track down his estranged son and heir, who for the last eight years was believed to have been wandering around the Himalayas. Accompanied by

Babaji, then fifty years old, as his guide and interpreter, Peabody eventually located Pfrumpy in a cave high up in the mountains of Ladakh, where he had apparently been living on his own for the last three years.

Pfrumpy and Babaji took an immediate liking to each other. According to Peabody, it was Babaji who had been instrumental in persuading Pfrumpy to come out of his cave to take up his duties at Pfrumpter Pharmaceuticals. Pfrumpy asked Babaji, some fifteen years his senior, if he would consent to return with him to Montreal as his private secretary, in fact he almost made Babaji's agreeing to do so a condition of coming out of his cave. Babaji prevaricated. Peabody, short of breath in the high altitude and shivering in the thin cotton safari suit he had bought for the Darjeeling climate, had even implored Babaji, close to tears. By Babaji's account, the comic aspect of the scene had suddenly struck the three of them after they had been parleying at the mouth of Pfrumpy's cave for the best part of a week – the portly little Indian and the shivering insurance agent, both of whom sorely missed their creature comforts, arguing vociferously outside the cave, the recalcitrant naked hermit, apparently immune to cold, thirst and hunger, no less vociferously inside – and they all started laughing.

These events had taken place twenty years ago.

Babaji brought Frank a cup of tea because he approved of Frank's presence in the house. He approved of the charity Pfrumpy and Wilma had shown Frank in offering him shelter. Living in a tent might be all right in Darjeeling but it was not the proper thing in Berlin. Babaji knew from Wilma about Frank but he didn't himself know Frank, indeed hadn't set eyes on him until he brought him his tea that morning. Babaji knew Wilma, of course, very well, and was extremely fond of her. It had not escaped him that the changes he had recently observed in Wilma, all of them to her advantage, from a general brightening of her mood down to the warmer skin tone in her usually rather pale complexion, had taken place since she began working with Frank and were therefore probably in some way due to Frank. All of this, and quite a lot more besides that would have eluded him had he tried to put it in words, found expression in the cup of tea Babaji brought Frank that morning.

CHAPTER
8.2

According to Babaji, in whom Wilma latterly confided almost more than in her husband, Wilma had begun to feel rather alone in the last three or four years of her marriage.

It was not as if anything had come between her and Pfrumpy. She had nothing to complain about. She was not dissatisfied, beyond an elusive feeling of discomfort. It just seemed to Wilma, in a vague but persistent way she had started to find irritating, that these days she had fewer things to look forward to than she had had when she met Pfrumpy twenty years previously.

Almost old enough to be her grandfather, as he often reminded her, perhaps with something else in mind, Babaji tried to comfort Wilma by telling her that with the twenty years of life behind her now which had still been in front of her then, well – there *were* fewer things to look forward to, such was the course of nature. And he quoted to her a poem by Gerard Manley Hopkins he had learned at school. Dedicated to a girl by the name of Margaret, the poem was a farewell written for the young child who has discovered death, recognising for the first time in the decaying autumnal world around her the paradigms of her own eventual extinction.

It *is* the blight man was born for,
It is Margaret you mourn for.

The phrase 'things to look forward to' had a particular connotation in Wilma's case.

Only seventeen, exactly half Pfrumpy's age when she met him on his return from Ladakh in 1970, Wilma was already something of a local celebrity in Montreal. As a high school volunteer for a series of ESP experiments carried out by researchers at Montreal's McGill University, Wilma was discovered to have an unusually developed gift for what was known as 'remote viewing'. She could describe 'blind' where someone was and in some cases what they were doing at locations she had never been to herself. This worked not just for sites in the Montreal area but for cities a few thousands miles away on the other side of the continent.[39]

Wilma's success at identifying remote viewing targets was coupled with a remarkable gift of *precognition*.

In the first tests, Wilma was only asked to 'view' and describe the location visited by one of the researchers when that person arrived there. However, as she grew familiar with the experimental procedure and more confident in her own skills, Wilma would feel impatient to 'take a look down the line', as she expressed it, and began viewing locations even before the control person had arrived there. The site was chosen by a random generator, the name of the site written down and sealed in an envelope to be picked up by any one of the dozen control persons who might be assigned to visit the site. It turned out Wilma was not merely able to describe the site before it was visited but *hours before it had even been chosen by the random generator*.

This gift of Wilma's remained an adjunct, as it were, of the experimental situation. She displayed it only when a skilful moderator led her on, asking the right kind of questions about a specific situation in the right way. Prescient though Wilma undoubtedly was, she could not foretell the future. Left to itself, the prescient faculty remained inert.

Throughout her training as a photographer and her early professional years doing fashion shoots, the faculty seemed to disappear entirely.

Wilma was unconcerned.

'It just comes and goes' she told her former moderator, who sought Wilma out in Toronto to find out what had happened to his teenage star. 'It does what it wants, not what *I* want. It really doesn't have an awful lot to do with me, you know.'

Then it was suddenly back.

For a week she stood in for a news photographer friend on the Toronto *Star* who had to leave town. It was a good week for news pictures – a plane crash on Lake Ontario, the biggest train wreck in the history of the province. In both cases, a very strong feeling 'came on' Wilma that she had to head down to the lake, take the highway north to a small-town railway crossing twenty miles outside the city limits. She reached both sites within minutes of the accident. Wilma's pictures for the *Star* scooped all the local media coverage, even made it onto TV.

As a freelance news photographer Wilma won national press Best Picture awards three years in succession before questions about the extraordinary coincidences her news scoops involved began to get embarrassing[40] and Wilma switched to less spectacular forms of photojournalism. Her knack of tracking down snow leopards and catching rare glimpses of gibbon inner family life led for a while to regular assignments for *National Geographic*, until mutterings in professional circles once again persuaded Wilma it might be better for her to move on.

She sought out her own subjects, individuals of no concern to the public beyond what Wilma managed to see in them, and in time found she was becoming not unlike them herself, vagrants in cities, children in refugee camps, students in communes. It was the latter that brought her to Berlin in November 1989, where Wilma arrived, how could it have been otherwise, the day before the Wall came down. Pfrumpy joined her for Christmas, rented a house, liked it there so much he made an offer the owner couldn't refuse, bought the house and stayed. A couple of months later, Wilma set foot in Potsdamer Platz just as Frank, Tom and Gerrit were beginning to pump out the cavernous puddle that had turned into a basilica before changing shape into a pissoir.

Bringing Frank into focus, still fifty yards away across that hopelessness of a square, still well ahead of Babaji remembering for her the poem he had learned at school in Darjeeling, Wilma found herself looking down the line at the blight man was born for, precognising what little of her slight self was left, a narrowing of the possibilities, children she with Pfrumpy had hoped for but were now resigned they would never have, and saw a thin frantic man with a long blonde mane of hair who seemed to her in his so evident fragility, his so clearly untenable position in that wasteland, to become less and less and less and less even during the few seconds it took her to adjust the shutter speed, and her heart went out to him, catching what little light was left at the close of an overcast winter day.

In this connection there was no escaping the size and general solidity of Pfrumpy. From Wilma's point of view, what she perceived as 'fragile' in Frank was seen against the background of Pfrumpy's 'solidity'. There was also the question of their respective ages. Frank was twelve years younger than Wilma, Pfrumpy seventeen years her senior, almost old enough, as Babaji would quite probably have also pointed out, to be her father.

Within the scenario of this entanglement, clearly there was chronological scope for Wilma to feature in quite a variety of roles – much broader than the variety available for men[41] – as mother, daughter, sister, wife. The family paradigm with its all too familiar role models was inescapable.

At the traditional Christmas party in his father's house when the recently returned prodigal son Pfrumpter Junior was first eased back into Montreal society, a quiet and rather solemn girl with American-Indian features[42] and one bristling jet-black braid of hair told him in the library about her experiences of remote viewing. One eye on the bristling braid of hair, half expecting it to rise and begin swaying like a charmed snake, Pfrumpy ran his hands across the spines of his father's books as he listened to the girl talk.

You saw just bits of things at first, she said, outlines and textures, something round or long, something dark, wet, dry, grainy, dense, a space. If the moderator asked the right questions, gradually the bits pieced together as elements of a recognisable picture. Often you had an urge to draw the picture rather than to try to describe it in words.

She could have dreams that were like remote viewing. Last night, for example, she dreamed she was in front of what she had taken at first to be a large telecast screen erected on the bank of a river. The river was there before the screen was. Then the screen took shape and gradually changed into a billboard. Words were written on it in a language she didn't understand. Pfrumpy wondered if she remembered the words and Wilma said she couldn't say the words, but she might be able to write them.

Pfrumpy asked her to write the words down in his address book. It was a short sentence in a language Pfrumpy didn't know either, but he thought Danish or perhaps Norwegian. He would find out. He asked her to add her phone number too. Because the felt-tipped pen he had given her to write with was drying up Wilma licked it, eking out enough ink for the last digits with a schoolgirl naturalness Pfrumpy found irresistible.

On his return from India Pfrumpy had gone back to college to take classes in chemistry and business administration at the same time Wilma began her course in photography. Their respective college buildings being located in the same small part of town, it was not surprising they bumped into each other quite often.

Meeting as students in a student milieu, getting nimbly in and out of each other's beds, Wilma was not bothered by the difference in their ages. She liked his candour. Pfrumpy told her exactly what he was thinking and often what she was thinking too. He seemed to know what was going on in her mind without her saying it. He knew when she was telling him one of her white lies, even the ones she told to herself. Faced with the complete lack of guile in Pfrumpy, Wilma dismantled the defences on which she ordinarily relied to protect her from getting hurt and entrusted herself to Pfrumpy without reserve.

In her role as the ward of the older man, Pfrumpy's daughter so to speak, Wilma enjoyed security. At the same time there was a lack of excitement about her relationship with Pfrumpy, something a bit too steady and middle-aged about it all, which only began to nag at Wilma when she was already engaged to him. There was already, in her early twenties, an inevitability to her future that Wilma found paralysing. There was all that money washing around in the Pfrumpter family that seemed to ridicule her own efforts at self-support. There was the certainty about Pfrumpy's patriarchal role as the head of the Pfrumpter family concern and fortune, and about the part his future spouse would play within it, down to the small print in the marriage contract Peabody & Son presented to Wilma, and which not even Pfrumpy could do anything about, specifying the respective percentages the aforesaid future spouse would receive as a personal annuity from the company in the event that she produced or failed to produce for it an heir.

Wilma broke off the engagement, escaped to Toronto and worked as a news photographer for the *Star*.

Living on her own in another city, Wilma found that she missed Pfrumpy more than she had expected. She missed having someone to talk to who understood her inside out and was able to make her feel calm. Her sometimes wordless conversations with Pfrumpy preceding this state of perfect calmness were among the happiest times in her life. They reminded Wilma of her contented mood as a child when she would hold a finger up to the sun and see the finger become transparent, as though a light went on inside her skin.

If, as Wilma acknowledged to herself, she missed Pfrumpy as the moving force of feelings that lit up inside her rather than as Pfrumpy in himself, a person existing outside her and having independent needs, was it just selfishness on her part? Did that matter? Could it have been otherwise? Obviously not, for who would the person have been that did not light her up inside? What private concern of hers would such a stranger be?

All of this made sense to Wilma. Feelings that lit up inside her as a recommendation of Pfrumpy seemed perfectly legitimate to her as an argument in favour of staying with him after all. Her side of it was clear.

Meanwhile, however, what did Pfrumpy miss?

Wilma wasn't quite sure. But oughtn't he, bringing in his complement, fulfilling his side of that ideal partnership she had constructed for them, miss Wilma lighting up for him as she missed being lit by him, and for better or worse perhaps the reverse of that too, casting the shadow that was first solicited by Pfrumpy's enabling light?

CHAPTER
8.31

'The basic force which gives rise to all these phenomena *(i.e. of quantum mechanics)* [43] is the force of electric attraction between the positively charged nucleus and the negatively charged electrons. It is responsible for all chemical reactions and for the formation of molecules. It is the basis for all solids, liquids and gases and all living organisms. The particle can no longer be seen as a static object but has to be conceived as a dynamic pattern. This new view was initiated by Dirac. The symmetry between matter and antimatter implies that for every particle there exists an antiparticle with equal mass and opposite charge.

The evidence seems to be that protons and neutrons, too, are composite objects; but the forces holding them together are so strong, or the velocities acquired by the components are so high, that the relativistic picture has to be applied, where the forces are also particles. Thus the distinction between the constituent particles and the particles making up the binding forces becomes blurred. The approximation of an object consisting of constituent parts breaks down.

All particles can be transmuted into other particles. They can be created from energy and vanish into energy, forming a web of inseparable energy patterns. Particles cannot be seen as isolated entities but as integrated parts of a whole. In a relativistic description of particle interactions – attraction or repulsion – are pictured as the exchange of other particles. Both force and matter are now seen to have their common origin in the dynamic patterns which we call particles.

In quantum field theories, the classical contrast between the solid particles and the space surrounding them is completely overcome. The quantum field is seen as the fundamental physical entity; a continuous medium which is present everywhere in space. Particles are merely local condensations of the field, concentrations of energy which come and go, thereby losing their individual character and dissolving into the underlying field. As Einstein says: 'We may therefore regard matter as being constituted by the regions of space in which the field is extremely intense . . . there is no place in this new kind of physics both for the field and matter, for the field is the only reality . . .'[44]

CHAPTER
8.4

Meanwhile, what did Pfrumpy miss?

Babaji's statement, made after her death, about Wilma having begun to feel rather alone in the last years of her marriage raises a number of problems.

Feelings may not be so easily divined as Babaji would have us believe, least of all by the person who has them. Whether Wilma truly felt 'alone' (whatever is meant by truly), or Babaji incorrectly inferred this from whatever she had told him, is a matter of conjecture. There is no record of what Wilma said to Babaji, and even if we had one — without a theory to establish a hypothesis about the nature of Wilma's feelings, it is impossible to determine what one is observing. *Pace* Einstein, and his advice to Heisenberg, it is impossible just to observe.

Like Babaji, Wilma only got to know the post-Ladakh Pfrumpy. Thirty-five years on, the sole traceable person still alive who knew Pfrumpy well both before his departure for India and after his return and ought thus to be in a position to give us an authentic picture of him was Lawrence Peabody.[45]

Pea went to high school with Pfrumpy and matriculated as a law student at Montreal University in the same year Pfrumpy was sent there by his father to study chemistry. Pfrumpy had no interest in studying chemistry. He had no interest in emulating his father. He was interested in girls, parties and golf. After his first year he dropped out of school. At the age of twenty-one, having come into the inheritance he had been left by his mother, killed in a car accident when he was only three, Pfrumpy was independently wealthy and could do as he pleased. He cocked a snook at his Dad and, apparently with great relish, set about frittering away his fortune and his youth. At twenty-four, Pfrumpy had an unchallenged reputation as the most eligible young bachelor alcoholic in town.

During the early 1960s, the Maharishi Mahesh began his rise to fame as the Indian sage best loved by the West. He toured the western world, draping himself with adoring celebrities like baubles. Pfrumpy caught the Maharishi, or the Maharishi caught him, on a snap visit to Hawaii where Pfrumpy happened to have gone on holiday. It was the turning point in his life. Before the Beatles set in motion a landslide of western youth to India, Pfrumpy had already entered a monastery in the remote valley of Zangskar in Ladakh, the Himalayan district of North West India bordering on Tibet.

Peabody didn't see Pfrumpy again until his journey to Zangskar with Babaji eight years later. Peabody's extraordinary judgement-day assessment of his childhood friend, quite outside the general consensus of opinion about Pfrumpy, has to be viewed in the context in which it was made, more than quarter of a century after the event and in the face of Peabody's early death from cancer only six months later.

According to his own diagnosis, Pea had failed in his life and he was dying not so much of cancer as of 'warping', what he called the 'metastases of envy' that Pfrumpy's existence had nourished in him more or less from the day he was born.

'Now this wasn't someone who had changed. This wasn't someone who was different from the person I had known before he left for India. This was a whole new person, *someone I had never met before*. It was actually a rather frightening experience for me. Please don't misunderstand me. During his eight years up there Pfrumpy had got very deep into religion, you know, all kinds of esoteric beliefs and practices, he'd acquired, I don't quite know how can one put this, certain, shall we say, *techniques*, giving him powers that were extraordinary, I mean, incredible. This new Pfrumpy who came out of the cave was without doubt a very *good* person. He was *kind*. He lived for other people, he really did. The hermit stayed in the cave and the man who came out of it returned to society and did good works for the remainder of his life. So it sounds like a cavil, it sounds ungenerous when I remind you that despite this new good person he'd undoubtedly become, Pfrumpy remained at bottom a reformed alcoholic, and as with all the reformed alcoholics I've known over the years it was the same in Pfrumpy's case, no exceptions, okay, so here's what I'm saying, the life spark seemed to have gone out of Pfrumpy, like a zombie, you know, a dead man resurrected but somehow not quite come back to life . . .'[46]

CHAPTER
8.41

In our notes towards a definition of Pfrumpy, we are left on the one hand with Peabody's extreme view of a 'zombie', on the other with a mixed bag of opinions about Pfrumpy regarding what one might neutrally describe as his very obvious standing-alone. They range from rather grand self-sufficiency to diffidence to an aloofness bordering on autism. Omit the grand and just call it self-sufficiency. This is the core. If we can venture a hypothesis as to the ground state of Wilma's feelings for Pfrumpy, it dates back to an insight she acquired in the period between breaking off her engagement and subsequently marrying him, namely, that Pfrumpy could not really miss her when she was separated from him in Toronto because he did not really need her when they were together in Montreal.

My first interviews with Pfrumpy were conducted at a time when I was considering a book about him, for which I had the tentative title *The biography of a CEO yogin*. I was then interested in the 'entanglement' of yoga and the successful business use Pfrumpy had made of it during his second lease of life as chairman of Pfrumpter Pharmaceuticals.

I found him perfectly approachable, but that already suggests the distance I was aware of having to reach over in my dealings with Pfrumpy. I sensed also that he was not very interested in the focus of my project, and I soon abandoned it. He rejected such categories as 'yogin' and 'CEO' because his philosophy subsumed all such categories in a non-differentiating involvement with whatever aspects of life. Pfrumpy's interest was in 'the bare forked animal'[47], and that interest was founded on the process of paradox, or what he called 'the eternal courtship of the poles dancing around the equator'[48].

That simile incidentally suggests why Pfrumpy preferred the more circumstantial expression 'process of paradox', – drawing out motion rather than stasis as implicit in the apparent fixedness of polarity, liquidity and fusion rather than a frozen state of separation, – to the simple word 'paradox'.

Among examples of processes of paradox that Pfrumpy collected in the book of commonplaces left among his papers[49] the subject of polar opposites was well represented. The image of the poles courting the equator found an echo in a quotation from that great physicist and meta-physicist Bohm.

'Consider the analogy of the poles of a magnet, which are a feature of linguistic and intellectual analysis and have no independent existence outside such analysis. At every part of a magnet there is a potential pair of north and south poles that overlap each other. But these magnetic poles are actually abstractions, introduced for convenience, while the whole process is a deeper reality – an unbroken magnetic field that is present over all space.'[50]

The marvellous writings of Bohm, whose master image of the universe as holograph served to bring out the symmetry of the whole reflected in its parts and the parts in the whole. Bohm's philosophy of an 'implicate order' that was quite similar to the Buddhist philosophy Pfrumpy had made his own during his retreat in the Himalayas, became a favourite source of contributions to the book of commonplaces.

Significantly, process-of-paradox entries were often paired. Thus, a characteristically exuberant pronouncement of Bohm's:–

'The notion of a separate organism is clearly an abstraction, as is also its *boundary*. Underlying all this is unbroken wholeness even though our civilisation has developed in such a way as to strongly emphasise the separation into parts.'[51]

– was tempered by the more sceptical and problematic intellect of the novelist Robert Musil, a mind perhaps even more labyrinthine than Bohm's:

'Everything exists through its *boundaries*[52], and therefore to some extent through an act of hostility to its surroundings. Thus one cannot dismiss out of hand that man's greatest bond with his fellow man lies in denying that bond and casting him off.'[53]

It may help to bear Musil's paradox in mind when reading the letter Pfrumpy in Montreal wrote to Wilma in Toronto, at a time when he knew he was at risk of losing Wilma and perfectly understood the reasons why.

What Pfrumpy missed was 'the bird'.

CHAPTER
8.411

'On the plank in the porch to the back, where you had the pots with the tomatoes last summer, the first snowdrift of the year has left a ledge about three inches deep. When I went out there in my pyjamas this morning I saw in the snow the claw marks of a bird. It had walked back and forth a couple of times and then flown off. I knew, of course, that it was you.

I put out seeds, hoping the bird would come back. It has since become a frequent guest.

The bird has shiny black feathers and bright black eyes and an indescribable morning smell. Beneath the morning freshness the smell has the remains of night in it, something acrid, maybe smoke, some not too clean corners of city masonry, moisture, something sweet.

In time, growing tame, it even hops up onto my finger and permits me to stroke its head. This has become quite a ritual between the two of us every morning, and there is a particular protocol that has to be followed.

It perches on my finger with its back to me and I stroke it, with my nose, downwards from the head to the tail. Then I do for the bird the same that I do for you on such occasions. I sniff the smooth black head. I nuzzle. I breathe in its odour and a pain in my heart causes me to sing, or whistle, or rather, since I can't really either sing or whistle, I purse my lips and suck in the air and make that sound you're familiar with, quite bird-like, a cheep when I get it right, a screech when I don't.

Well, this bird that is you or this you that is the bird recognises the sound — improbable and even ridiculous as it may seem — to be a love call. It knows these vibrations in the air are terms of endearments. It hears the unspeakable. These are the audible vibrations of an otherwise speechless heart. There is no one else to whom the call can be addressed, no other being to hear it, which is why the bird does me the kindness of coming back again and again to listen, does itself that kindness, for how could there be a sound separated from its listener, or a listener separated from its sound?'[54]

About six months after Lawrence Peabody's inconclusive visit to Berlin he sent me a CD-Rom and asked me for my comments on it, 'our little experiment', as he called it. In the covering letter he explained that on his return to Montreal he had turned over to the experts in Pfrumpy's insurance company's research department all the data he had collected in Berlin, with a request for an analysis of the accident on Glienicker Bridge, or failing that, at least a working hypothesis. The experts had been unable to meet either of these requests to his satisfaction.

The analysis took the form of a computer animation. In a series of still images, it first showed the bridge over the Havel from a variety of angles, from below, from above, from both sides, from either end, with precise measurements of whatever we were looking at. It explored, in particular detail, the gap in the steel balustrade through which the car had plunged into the river.

Metallurgists had been put to work on a sample of the section of the balustrade. They had analysed the steel alloy of which it was made, opening up an arcane world of things hidden from the normal observer, such as the alloy's crystal structure, what the specialists called the timelines of its fatigue history, its yield stress, ultimate tensile stress, and so on.

Given a balustrade made of this alloy with these properties and built to the specifications of the Glienicker Bridge, the metallurgists calculated it would have required a projectile with the weight of Pfrumpy's car to have been travelling at a velocity around 45–50 kph to have torn so cleanly through the balustrade and landed at the spot in the river from which it had been retrieved, some forty metres from the bridge.

This was a purely theoretical calculation, however, based on a collision between the balustrade and an object impacting it *head-on*. Such a speed could only have been reached by a car accelerating as it crossed the bridge, but then, as it were, *changing its mind*, being compelled to make a sudden left-hand turn at an angle approaching ninety degrees to achieve a clean exit from the bridge. In this case the car would have overturned and conceivably gone over the bridge backwards. The nature of the damage done to the car and the bridge, the lack of marks on the surface of the road, and so on, ruled out any such scenario.

In whatever way one explained the behaviour of a projectile travelling at the kind of speed needed to create forces of the magnitude that had evidently been at work here, there might be a quite simple explanation for the considerable distance it had travelled after breaking through the balustrade. It need not have 'flown' the fifty metres from the bridge to the site from which it was salvaged. It could have swum there, the experts thought, bumped along the river bed by the strong current apparent at this point on the Havel where a relatively narrow, marginally higher water course disgorged into a lower lake-like expanse.

In a technical appendix to these findings my attention was drawn to a diagram showing the crystal structure of the steel alloy of the balustrade. It showed, greatly magnified, a microscopic crack, described as a potential *initiation site*. Whether or not it became one in actuality was a different matter. In my mind this rang a bell. Probabilistically, such initiation sites represented a weak point in the structure of the balustrade, a danger spot, even 'a concealed hole', as it was represented in the graphics of the CD-Rom, its presence on the bridge highlighted by a faint luminous glow.

On a mild spring day in late March I cycled out to Glienicker Bridge. Just a few years after unification of the country, there was nothing there to remind one of the border the bridge had once marked. Only six months after the accident, there was nothing to remind one of the events of that night either. The bridge had since been overhauled. I could no longer say for sure at what exact point the car had plunged off.

I leaned over the balustrade, dropped a stick into the river and watched it rotating slowly on its own axis. Then I wandered down to the Potsdam end of the bridge and looked back.

This was the view you got in the final motion picture sequence that reconstructed the accident on the CD-Rom. After all the facts and the various analyses of them had been presented, the best that Peabody's team could come up with was a black-and-white cartoon strip conclusion, a science fiction anti-climax to the scientific investigation Peabody had commissioned.

In the end sequence you became Pfrumpy's co-driver. Briefly you saw him in profile. Then you turned and saw through the windscreen what he saw, an empty blackness only defined as a road by its white border. You straightened out of the curve and saw the bridge ahead of you. It seemed more like tunnel vision than the view of a bridge. All you really saw was lightness at the end of the tunnel, marking the exit at the far end of the bridge, and a flickering luminescence about halfway down on the left, representing the 'concealed hole', the gap in the girders and the potentially weak section in the balustrade through which the car would pass.

In the next image you lost the frame of the windscreen you had been looking through, giving you the impression that the car had passed on without you, through you, and left you standing at the entrance to the bridge. You waited a few seconds, curious to watch the trajectory of the car as it entered your field of vision and went over the bridge, but you didn't see the car, just a flaring up of the luminescent spot on the left of the screen, a sudden burst of brilliant light, then a whiteout, no recognisable contours, nothing.

I wandered back to the spot where I had left my bicycle on the bridge, and stood for a few minutes in the sunshine, leaning on the balustrade as I admired the view. In the river just below me, the stick I had dropped there half an hour before was still rotating lazily on the eddies under the bridge.

It seemed very familiar. All you really saw was lightness at the end of the tunnel, representing the exit at the far end of the bridge, and a flickering luminescence drawing attention to the 'concealed hole' on the left, effectively a second exit. While I was cycling back I gradually realised what the set-up in the CD-Rom simulation reminded me of. It was the darkened box I had peered into as a physics student. What it reminded me of was the double-slit experiment.

CHAPTER
10

Frank's seven-ton steel Bar was in storage in a disused bus depot in East Berlin. A couple of days before Reunification Day, or Unification Day, as some of us preferred to call it (what could there possibly be back there that anyone wanted to put together again?) a group of friends from the Institute went round to take a look at it.

All East Berliners who had visited the Palace of the Republic (and at some point in our lives just about all of us had) could claim a former acquaintance with the Bar. Not as patrons – sitting and being served at the Bar had been reserved for the *nomenklatura*, Presidium members and their families, high-ups in the Party – but tourists, admirers from afar as we were ushered past the VIP cordon that separated us from our leaders on our way into the gigantic auditorium.

Standing in a corner surrounded by the junk of old diesel engines, wrapped in potato sacks which Frank swept aside, the magnificent organ-pipe-mantled bar seemed so humiliated in these surroundings that even Sichrovsky, even Ulla, who had suffered under the old regime and hated almost everything associated with it, admitted to a pang of something like bitterness when they saw how far this monument to Socialist Art had come down in the world. We would go along out of solidarity, but we really didn't need to see Frank's installation with the Bar on the bank of the Spree. We had already got the point in the bus depot.

Thousands of celebrations, tens of thousands of parties were held all over the country on Unification Day. On a single day more money was spent on booze and fireworks than was traditionally spent over the entire Christmas and New Year holiday. It was above all the boozers and firebrands on both sides of the former border who found themselves sentimentally reunited around tribal hearths in ancient forests that day.

Frank's installation on the bank of the river within sight of the Palace of the Republic was intended to appeal to a more discriminating clientele. Designed by Frank and documented by Wilma, it was paid for by Pfrumpy, their first collaboration, the first joint statement issued to the public by the troika living in the tree-lined street off the Q-Damm.

The large old house was the only building on the block to have survived the wartime bombs. It had acquired a certain local notoriety during the year the Pfrumpters and Babaji had been living there. Wilma came and went at all hours in her Arafat headgear and desert camouflage fatigues, sometimes on a bicycle, sometimes in a Porsche. Pedestrians on their way to work came to recognise the portly little Indian by his surprisingly delicate ankles and white-soled dark brown feet, visible, indeed sometimes even seeming to wave at passers-by through the window, for the ten minutes each morning when Babaji was inverted, standing on his head on the sitting-room carpet with his legs in the air.

Upstairs, on a tiny terrace niched into the Wilhelmian gable-windowed roof in full view of employees of the Bleibtreu Insurance offices across the street, the master of the house performed his yoga meditations, stark naked even in the middle of winter.

Arriving at the beginning of one of the most frantic and emotional years in the history of the German people, Pfrumpy found himself drawn somewhat against his disengaged nature into the events taking place around him. He was at an age too, when questions about his family origins that until now had never interested him began to trickle into his consciousness. When he tracked down a clock-making great-grandfather who had left Neu-Cölln in the nineteenth century and emigrated to Canada Pfrumpy felt, as he remarked to Babaji, more secure, as if a loose end of him that had been flapping around in the dark had finally been made fast. It was under the influence of all these events that Pfrumpy rented a country house in a little place called Holm where he and Wilma would spend the following three summers.

The trip to Berlin was one he had long been planning to make.

Having fulfilled, or almost fulfilled, the pledge he had made to Peabody outside the cave in Ladakh to devote twenty years of his life to Pfrumpter Pharmaceuticals and then step down, his departure for Berlin 'on holiday' the previous November had already indicated his readiness to go. Eleven months later, it must have become clear to everyone back home that at least in his capacity as CEO of a company in Montreal Pfrumpy had gone for good, leaving behind him a corporate-duty public-figure life to which he did not ever intend to return.

There were plenty of precedents for taking such a step in the country that still claimed Pfrumpy's spiritual allegiance. Indian businessmen going into retirement might still substitute begging bowl for briefcase and set out on the road with their pilgrim's staff. But in Berlin?

CHAPTER
10.1

When asked this question in one of his more malicious moods it could amuse Pfrumpy to deliver a long, excruciatingly detailed lecture to his interlocutors, laying it on with a trowel, walling them in with his erudition in a matter of no conceivable interest to anyone except Buddhist scholars. He could talk by the hour about the late nineteenth-century discovery made by the sinologist Rosencrantz of a cache of Buddhist manuscripts in a cave in Dunhuang, China.

Now this *Rosencrantz*, said Pfrumpy — and when he leaned in over a captive audience from his towering height he could make this very Jewish name sound like Frankenstein, some Holocaust-avenging doom[55] — had got to the cave in Dunhuang before his much more famous colleague *Stein*, but this had remained unknown in the West. The Rosencrantz manuscripts were transported back to Berlin and, under conditions of secrecy as impermeable as they were inexplicable, unless perhaps as a symptom of Rosencrantz' *paranoid personality*, they joined the archives of the Oriental Institute at the Kaiser Wilhelm University, later Humboldt, in what became known as East Berlin.

During the war, the manuscripts were apparently removed for safekeeping. They had never been seen since. As all the catalogues of the Institute went up in flames with the rest of the building, not a scrap of evidence had survived establishing even the bare existence of the manuscripts. Pfrumpy, however, had in his possession a letter Rosencrantz had written to a colleague in Vienna at the time of his extraordinary discovery in Dunhuang. The wording of the letter was so close to Stein's account of the Dunhuang caves twenty years later that

Stein might almost have been quoting Rosencrantz, although he maintained he had never even heard of his obscure predecessor.

'Our manuscripts are from a collection taken from the walled up small room connected to the side of a cave shrine at the Caves of the Thousand Buddhas. A hoard of paintings were packed together on a vast scale, neatly enough to suggest a repository of sacred material no longer in use rather than a hurried stash sparked by an invasion of the area. At the time the room was sealed the Tibetan manuscripts would have had little practical use yet they form the largest amount of material, at least by bulk, greater than the Chinese. Equally there were a number of things stored away which were in effect no more than sacred rubbish – carefully sewn up small bags of tiny scraps of inscribed paper, silk tapes, cloth wrappers and the like. It seems reasonable to assume that our manuscripts, found amongst this material, were either written at or brought to Dunhuang sometime in the late eighth or early ninth century.'

'I had heard from a trader about a rumour of this hidden deposit of manuscripts in one of the caves among the Caves of the Thousand Buddhas south-east of Dunhuang. The Daoist priest, Wang Yuanlu, had organised the restoration of one of the larger shrines and during the cleaning of sand and debris from the cave temple a crack was noticed in a frescoed wall. Investigation uncovered the room, filled with packets of manuscripts, Sanskrit, Chinese, Khotanese, Sogdian, Uigur, and Tibetan. The sealed room was good for preservation as it would have had a steady temperature, it was absolutely dry, and the thinnest wall, the walled up entrance to the room, was covered by drifting sand for centuries. On the expedition which conveyed our manuscripts back to Berlin, about 500 paintings on silk, linen and paper, and about 6500 manuscripts and printed books were brought back from the Caves of the Thousand Buddhas and presented to the Oriental Institute of the Humboldt University . . . .'[56]

And so on and so forth.

This business about Rosencrantz and his lost manuscripts being the reason why Pfrumpy settled in Berlin never convinced me. I always felt that Pfrumpy was putting one over on us, or at least holding something back.

When Pfrumpy first heard from Wilma of the exploits of Basilica Frank, this urban pot-holer's evident familiarity with Berlin's underground labyrinth in the sandy soil beneath the city impressed him. No doubt the sand here was just as good as in Dunhuang, fine-grained, dry, as well suited for the preservation of manuscripts as for gunpowder. Pfrumpy became excited. Almost certainly this was where the Rosencrantz manuscripts had gone into storage. Frank would be the man who would find them for him. What Frank and Wilma had subsequently found on the twenty-sixth subterranean level beneath Tempelhof airport was not the discovery Pfrumpy had envisaged.

CHAPTER
10.12

But meanwhile Unification intervened, and for several weeks on either side of it Frank's attention was monopolised by the Bar. He had plans for the Bar. He wanted to send it on a world tour, to exhibit the steel beast at Grand Central Station in New York, at the Hagia Sophia in Istanbul, climactically on Ayer's Rock down under. With a little help from Pfrumpy....but although Pfrumpy agreed it was an interesting idea, he wasn't sure about the Bar taking off inside the Haga Sophia, let alone on Ayer's Rock. He wasn't sure people there would appreciate it.

Try it out here first, advised Pfrumpy. Give it a local run.

Frank obtained a dozen naked men, a dozen full-body plastic mouldings from Dressman Ltd., suppliers to the tailoring industry, and a dozen chrome and leather bar stools left over from the sale of the inventory of the Palace of the Republic. These articles were delivered to the house during the mid-morning coffee break of the Bleibtreu Insurance secretaries. Looking down they were able to see Frank, Wilma and Babaji in the downstairs room across the street, laying the dozen naked Dressman dummies in a line on the floor, adjusting their limbs, if necessary with force, before making them respectable in a dozen identical office-grey suits. Wilma stepped back to take photos. Babaji opened cartons of paper clips, ball-point pens, screwed up balls of paper and what appeared to be sackfuls of coins and paper money. All these things were stuffed to bursting into the pockets of the suits. The twelve grey-suited men were then carried outside, loaded into a removals van and driven away.

At the bus depot, Frank and Jeronimus glued them to the stools by their seat bottoms, lashed the stools to the bar and covered the whole thing with a tarpaulin. There they remained under wraps until the dawn of Unification Day.

Frank sat in a bar drinking beer with Jeronimus, explaining to him the idea behind his installation. Frank talked. The pastor listened, nodded at intervals, wiped the foam out of his moustache and said nothing.

The last-minute involvement of Pastor Jeronimus was instigated by Pfrumpy. Until then, Frank had been intending to deliver the loudspeaker commentary at the scene of his installation. Pfrumpy persuaded him this was not a good idea. Moral indignation was unbecoming in anyone but an East Berliner, somebody known to have been a victim of the old regime, who had the right to speak out. Such opposition as was possible under that regime had been led by people of the Church. Among them the name of Pastor Jeronimus, who had been sent to prison for his outspoken views, was especially prominent.

The Lutheran pastor exemplified a headstrong, hungry-looking, schismatic breed of men whose fiery spirit did justice to the founder of their religion. Almost overnight they had sprung up around the country, these wild-eyed, long-haired and very timely apostolic figures who stepped forward to become the saviours in the ruins all around them. It was not socialism they condemned, but its corruption. Even as they poured scorn into the ears of their congregations, denouncing the venality of the politicians, they remained the defenders of the socialist faith. There was still some good there, they insisted, something worth hanging onto in the headlong embrace with their capitalist brethren. This crumb of comfort, this remnant of self-respect they had restored to a thoroughly demoralised people, gave anchorage to the moral authority with which men like Pastor Jeronimus were endowed.

On a windy, cloud-chasing afternoon the pastor stood with Frank's party of invited guests on the platform erected on the Museumsinsel within sight of the Palace of the Republic, where the Bar had until recently been housed. A crowd of several thousand spectators stood around them on the banks of the Spree. All heads upturned as a giant hydraulic arm lifted the Bar in its claw, extended the arm to its maximum reach, and stopped at a height of some thirty metres above the river. The crowd hushed. There the Bar hung, complete with the twelve grey-suited figures on stools lashed lengthways along either side.

Slowly the claw twisted, moved through ninety degrees until the Bar stood vertical in the air, turned it upside down and began to shake it.

The whole huge machine shuddered. A head fell off. One of the dummies came unstuck and plunged down. The Bar vibrated in the grip of the claw. A slow whispering shower of objects, the ill-gotten gains that had been pocketed by the representatives of the people, made plopping sounds as they pitted the surface of the river. Bundles of notes, blank pieces of paper and counterfeit money scattered by the wind, descended from the sky. The crowd made a grab for it, fought over it, laughed and howled. In ten minutes the spectacle was over. Jeronimus stepped forward to the microphone. Silence fell.

– Am I my brother's keeper?

The pastor paused for a minute. The crowd stood rooted in absolute silence.

– Not all their names are recorded. I have here, on the list I am going to read to you, the names of five hundred and eleven people who during the twenty-nine years from August 13th 1961 to November 9th 1989 are known to have been shot while they were trying to cross the border between East and West Berlin. Many others were killed whose names are not known, let alone remembered. Many thousands more were imprisoned.

A ripple passed through the crowd, a sort of collective sigh. Day was drawing in as the pastor began to read the list of names. By the time he was done, an hour later, it was already dark, and the sporadic sounds that at first might have been mistaken for distant gun shots became a constant barrage, blossoming into a gaudy tracery of fireworks, illuminating the night sky all around us.

Came the reckoning.

When the archives of the Secret Police were opened, citizens of the deceased Republic could apply for permission to inspect whatever files had been kept on them. Hordes of applicants descended on the office in East Berlin, hour-long queues formed outside. Many went home empty-handed, disappointed to learn that they had not been considered a sufficient security risk to warrant keeping a file on them.

A population that had only recently been reunited soon found itself divided into first and second class citizens, those with a file and those without.

In our house, all the members of Ulla's and Peter's kitchen cabinet had a file, only the old couple who lived in the basement had got by without one.

How to find the words for the horrors this file contained?

An outside observer, perhaps from Frank's point of view, might tell it like this.

Imagine you went to the seaside and the sea was empty. Imagine you woke up one morning, like Gregor Samsa, and found yourself turned into a beetle, or just looked into the mirror and saw someone else's face looking back.

Imagine you walked to the Brandenburg Gate and there was a wall blocking your path, and east was divided from west Berlin. Imagine you went back there thirty years later, and the wall had gone.

Berlin was the city of metamorphosis, illusion, counterfeit. It now wasn't the Berlin it once used to be. It was a brand name, disguising a different product. The city changed, while the name remained the same, like Peter, the name for a person of as diverse aspects as a holding company. Peter should have had different names, a directory in which to look him up, so that one knew what line of Peter one was dealing in.

The passport giving the ID of the Peter we knew was a notepad always on the kitchen table, covered with mathematical symbols. His wife Ulla, large and plentiful, physically and figuratively, was Peter's 'better half', said this lean poorer-half Peter whom we knew. They had always been church and protest people, as everyone now was, had become overnight, in East Berlin. All East Berliners were covering their tracks. The three of us sat in the kitchen and talked and talked. This was practical talk. The politics of the day. For the first time things were actually happening. Not might or could, the inch work of the tiniest, most marginal improvements to be wrung from the old state we had grown up with, but differences as bold as night and day, changing the world, it seemed, at a stroke.

When Ulla went to bed, or when Peter, Frank and I went round the block for a drink, it was the turn of impractical talk. Bell's Theorem, entanglement, quantum mechanics. Peter elaborated on Dirac's theory of anti-matter. He had been working around this subject for the last ten years.

We would play with the theory. In a universe opposite to the one in which Isaac Newton observed a falling apple, did the apple necessarily rise, or did it merely not fall? And what about anti-Newton?

Frank reduced the theory to accommodate the special case of Berlin. He imagined one half of the city as Berlin, the other as anti-Berlin. Everything on one side of the wall had its mirror image, its opposite on the other. The Wall itself illustrated Frank's mirror image idea perfectly. In one Berlin, the Wall had kept people out who didn't want to come in. In the other, it had kept people in who wanted to get out[57].

Frank was an insomniac. He occupied himself with trivial pursuits of matter versus anti-matter as a way of getting to sleep at night. He was intrigued by the subject of opposites. Windows and curtains. Facades, behind facades.

Closed files in ministries in East Berlin gradually began to be opened. Totalitarian, democratic. Stooge, anti-stooge. Good, bad. Impractical talk began to get a word in edgeways on practical talk. The matter/anti-matter debate became headline news in the tabloid press. A German proneness to polarisation followed with renewed vigour on the truce that had been briefly called after unification.

It was Pfrumpy who showed Frank how, in a state of meditation, one could concentrate on black and white until one no longer saw any difference between them. But completeness required this difference. Black and white enabled one another and resided in one entity[58]. Everything needed an opposite to be itself[59]. There was an apparently unavoidable element of reconciliation, of peacekeeping, in this compromise of warring opposites to find the middle truth.

CHAPTER
10.1211

Frank, Wilma and Pfrumpy went on holiday in Italy.

Moist fall dulled the splintering sounds in Berlin when they came back in early November, a year after the fall of the Wall, and sat at the breakfast table reading the *Berliner Morgenpost*. The paper was full of breakage. Splinters lay all over the floor. You had to watch where you stepped. The lead story was about a mathematician named Peter, who on behalf of the East German ministry of state security had spied on his wife Ulla for the last twenty years.

Baffled, unbelieving, Frank sought them out in their run-down apartment behind Potsdamer Platz. To some extent he went out of sympathy, but the larger part may have been curiosity. What would it be like?

It was like a couple on holiday in a run-down seaside resort, looking out of the window in the morning to find the sea gone.

'It's just not possible,' said Ulla.

Peter didn't say anything.

On the morning after the story broke in the *Morgenpost* Peter had woken up and found himself transformed into a beetle with a hard shiny carapace.

Peter realised he was loathsome. There was *the thing* about him. He gnawed the ends of his fingers and didn't say anything. He had forfeited the right to speech, because never, ever ever ever, was anyone ever going to believe in Peter again.

He sat in the darkness in the children's bedroom (the children had been sent away to stay with Ulla's sister in the country), just like Gregor Samsa become beetle[60], with the door ajar to the living room, where Ulla sat talking with me and Frank. She could feel his presence through the crack in the door, a cold dark effluence that was Peter.

Ulla went through phases of shock.

The first phase was believing it must all be a mistake. The sea was not empty, it was there, she just couldn't see it. The soundtrack to Phase One was 'It's just not possible,' which she repeated to herself time after time, her liturgy of unbelief, as she sat with her legs under her, keening, rocking back and forth. At such moments, I thought of Ulla as performing some ritual ablution in a clearing in a forest, to ward off the darkness that streamed into the clearing where Ulla, surrounded by forces of forest darkness, was struggling for light.

There followed speechlessness, enforced, active silence in which many words were spoken and always cancelled each other out. Ulla exclaimed. She got up, no, she was wrested from the floor by an invisible hand that plucked her up and shook her. The force of unspoken words inside her snapped her out of the trance.

Words not said became things she did. She got tough. She became violent. She hit him.

She wanted an explanation, something that would help her to stay alive.

'Why did he do it, Frank?' she asked, not expecting from him an answer.

Her first, brief interrogation of her husband had yielded an astonishing idea, so peculiar that Ulla hadn't even heard it. Now she returned to it, picked it up, a cat with a dead mouse in her jaws, shook it ragged.

— What he told me was . . . .

Ulla shook her head and wept, the first tears.

What Peter had told her was that he had spied on her to protect her. This needed a little elaboration.

Ulla had joined the church/protest movement long before there was any sign of the political system in East Germany collapsing. She had lived dangerously. The protest groups were under blanket surveillance, round the clock. The people who did the surveillance were themselves under surveillance by others. It was Peter's notion that the deeper he blended into this many-layered structure of totalitarian control, moving between surface and depth, living the officially approved life of deception, there was a chance of being able to influence it from within. He would be able to see his wife as the enemy saw her. Peter would be Ulla's early-warning system.

We imagined Peter, the matter/anti-matter theoretician on his way to work in the morning. Bye, Ulla. Peter kissing his wife as he left the house. Sitting at a desk in his office at the Humboldt, covering sheets of paper with hieroglyphs, strolling out for lunch, sandwiches punctually on a park bench. Fellow came and sat down beside him, a rolled newspaper under his arm.

So how was the wife keeping? Momentarily the theoretician might have been thrown by this harmless inquiry. Which one? The wife or the anti-wife?

Was it a bit like having an affair with a woman that he kept secret from Ulla? Had it given him a thrill?

— No.

Peter frowned, adjusting his spectacles higher on his nose, but not in order to look at us.

— Not a bit like that.

For a while Peter went to stay with Wilma and Pfrumpy, because Ulla said she couldn't stand him in the house. There was nowhere else for him to go.

The argument against Peter's claim that he had spied on his wife for her own benefit was that in the end it hadn't done her much good. In the end the communists chucked her out. For the last twelve months of the rotten Republic, Ulla had lived in exile in the other Germany.

Peter's spin to the argument was that the outcome would have been much worse if he hadn't spied on her. Then Ulla would have gone to prison. Peter had kept her out of prison by presenting her subversive life to the secret police in such a way that she was considered a suitable candidate for the chuck-'em-out as opposed to the lock-'em-up treatment.

The notion that Ulla, given the option, might have preferred to go to prison and not have her husband spy on her, was not one that Peter had entertained. On the contrary, Peter showed no sign of remorse. He was a hard-liner. He wasn't sorry for what he had done because he still thought it had been the right thing to do. He still believed in Communism. Even as the ground was opening under his feet and gobbling Communists up, he still insisted he had betrayed his wife for love of her, because he cared about her well-being.

How long was he going to stay with them, Wilma asked Pfrumpy. He gave her the creeps. She wished he'd go.

But Pfrumpy was fascinated by Peter. It was like having a monster, Gregor Samsa turned beetle, living with them in the house. The anti-Peter had been spawned. Not just a different personality, a person who acted differently, but Peter's opposite number, the anti-Peter who cancelled Peter out.

Cancelled Ulla out, too.

Ulla was as neat and tidy and complete a work of destruction as anything I had ever seen. There wasn't much to show for it on the outside. Peter's betrayal had made a tiny prick in her heart, so painlessly that Ulla hadn't even noticed, inserted a tube, and sucked out her insides, turning her into a zombie. She became anti-Ulla, the walking dead, moved to another city, changed her name, disappeared from the horizon of our lives.

Peter, or anti-Peter, moved into another apartment, continued to work on Dirac's theory at Humboldt University, took his sandwiches out to the park for lunch. His presence as an observer on the team of Sichrovsky's project was no longer needed. We lost sight of Peter too, whoever Peter was.

CHAPTER
II

'The paradox of Einstein, Podolsky and Rosen,' opened John S.Bell's famous paper of that title which appeared in *Physics, 1* in 1964, 'was advanced as an argument that quantum mechanics could not be a complete theory but should be supplemented by additional variables. These additional variables were to restore to the theory causality and locality. In this note[61] that idea will be formulated mathematically and shown to be incompatible with the statistical predictions of quantum mechanics. It is the requirement of locality, or more precisely that the result of a measurement on one system be unaffected by operations on a distant system with which it has interacted in the past, that creates the essential difficulty.'

As observers of a thought experiment earlier proposed by Bohm and Aharanov to illustrate the Einstein-Podolsky-Rosen (EPR) argument[62], we are invited by Bell 'to consider a pair of spin one-half particles formed somehow in the singlet spin state and moving freely in opposite directions. Measurements can be made, say by Stern-Gerlach magnets, on selected components of the spins 0_1 and 0_2. If measurement of the component 0_1 yields the value $+1$ then, according to quantum mechanics, measurement of 0_2 must yield the value -1 and vice versa. Now we make the hypothesis...that if the two measurements are made at places remote from one another the orientation of one magnet does not influence the result obtained with the other. Since we can predict in advance the result of measuring any chosen component of 0_2 by previously measuring the same component of 0_1, it follows that the result of any such measurement must actually be predetermined.'[63]

Heisenberg's Uncertainty Principle implies that it is possible to know the spin value of a particle along *only one axis at a time*. Also, in a pair of entangled particles like the two spin one-half particles in the experiment discussed in §5, the spin values would *always be correlated*. If the spin measured along the x-axis of O_1 yielded a value $+1$, the corresponding spin of O_2 must automatically have a value of -1. By the same token, EPR proposed that it should be possible to take also a second measurement at the very same instant as the first, for example a spin of $+1$ along the y-axis of O_2, and thus know, without needing to measure it, that the corresponding spin value of O_1 must be -1. But according to quantum mechanics, this second measurement was not possible. It was categorically ruled out by the Uncertainty Principle.

A further difficulty with the quantum mechanical prediction regarding the correlation of entangled particles was that the correlation would hold true irrespective of the distance between them. As Bell states above: 'It is the requirement of locality, or more precisely that the result of a measurement on one system be unaffected by operations on a distant system with which it has interacted in the past, that creates the essential difficulty.'

For how could entangled particles perhaps separated from their partners by millions of light years 'know' instantaneously what the other was doing? How could a transmission of information take place exceeding the speed of light?

The obvious way round these difficulties, suggested by EPR and taken up by Bell, was to assume that 'the result of any such measurement must actually be predetermined.' The particles in question must be supposed to possess more variables than had so far been accounted for by quantum mechanics. Being unknown, they were termed 'hidden variables.'

EPR's twin premises of locality and hidden variables lead to the formulation of Bell's Inequality. Given those twin premises, Bell's Inequality states what correlations between two systems separated in space are to be expected. Quantum mechanical calculations lead theoretically to predictions of correlations, for example between the spins of the particles, which would violate Bell's Inequality.

Experiments by Aspect and others, of the kind outlined here and above in §5, causing entangled particles to travel in opposite directions until they encounter analyzers that measure the spin component of the particles at different angles, do indeed establish correlations between those measurements that violate Bell's Inequality[64].

How then could EPR's two assumptions of locality and determinism be upheld? One of them would have to be dropped. Bell himself was among those in favour of dropping locality, opening a door to some non-local form of synchronicity of events separated across unbounded time and space, setting loose a host of speculations about interdependence of mind and matter in an entangled universe; a modus operandi rejected by Einstein as 'spooky action at a distance' taking place (if it took place at all) outside the known laws of physics.

Einstein's position that a particle must have a separate reality independent of measurement would be shaken. The very notion of such a reality would be shaken. Perhaps it was with such consequences in mind that Stapp judged Bell's Theorem to be 'the most profound discovery of science'.

Sichrovsky, his assistant Jens, Frank and I met with a reluctant liaison officer from the defunct Ministry of State Security, an official from the Ministry of Research and Technology in Bonn and the two telecommunications experts they had brought with them from former East and West Berlin respectively, in the basement of a house off Potsdamer Platz. For ten years prior to the fall of the Wall it had served the Ministry of State Security as a listening post right on the doorstep of West Berlin.

On the outside, the building was just another down-and-out, a derelict like all the uninhabited houses surrounding it. There was no hint of what went on in the basement. The entrance to the house had been sealed. Access to the basement had been gained via a tunnel that surfaced in a building some fifty metres away. There was a sort of vestibule you passed through when you emerged from the tunnel, fitted out as a lugubrious shrine to the ancestral gods of State Security. A bust of Dzerzhinsky[65], founding father of the modern security police agency, stood beside a vase of plastic flowers in a niche, illuminated by a queasy-making violet-coloured light. The bookshelves beneath housed the complete works of the Cheka, twenty or thirty volumes bound in suitably blood-red leather.

Traces of a hurried departure from the basement were still in evidence, twelve months later. The Citizens Committee on guard here had made sure that nothing was tampered with. A faint smell of burning hung in the passage. It came from a room at the end, where an open door revealed an incinerator and piles of documents there had not been enough time to burn. Other doors opened into rooms stocked with alcohol, cigarettes, chocolates and canned food that had been mailed from the West to relatives in the East only to have it purloined by State Security for officially sanctioned private consumption.

The first hostilities were opened in the passage before we had even reached the communications room that was the purpose of our visit. Sichrovsky stopped and stared at the piles of confiscated goods on the shelves.

– I always wondered about those food parcels with the *foie gras* my aunt in Strasbourg used to send me for Christmas. Only one of them ever reached me. So while I . . . my aunt and I wondered . . . the *foie gras* . . . you know, all the while these gentlemen from the State Security were merrily helping themselves . . . , the pigs . . . absolutely outrageous . . . how dare they, the thieving communist swine!

The words 'these gentlemen' were offloaded with heavy sarcasm on the East Berlin liaison officer who had been assigned to show us round the premises. 'These gentlemen' shrugged his shoulders, mumbled something unintelligible and busied himself with opening up the heavy lead-plated door that sealed the communications room from external wave interference. As for the thieving communist swine, he had already moved away and turned his back on any swine that might be around and mistaken for him, making plain he had nothing to do with them at all.

We followed him into a small, overcrowded room that smelt of sweat and a more general brew of indefinable staleness. After a minute the atmosphere was already stifling. Requested to switch on the air conditioning, the liaison officer told us that there wasn't any. The walls all round appeared to be armour-plated, insulated with lead or some metal alloy to prevent detection by the same kind of equipment on the far side of the Wall that was assembled here, only it looked second-hand, if not to say obsolete, and was stamped with Cyrillic letters. Probably it had been the standard outfitting for decoding rooms in all Soviet embassies abroad.

The bulky man from the ministry in Bonn squeezed into one of the cockpit-style cable-wreathed booths and attempted to sit down.

– It must have got rather hot and sticky in here. Rather claustrophobic. You had shifts working down here all round the clock? You poor devils, you must have been sweating like pigs.

The liaison officer, hearing the word 'pig' for the second time in as many minutes, responded with what was evidently the all-purpose gesture of the day, another of his wordless shrugs.

– Get anything useful out of this....lot?

The man from the ministry in Bonn waved impatiently at the equipment as if the liaison officer were a waiter being instructed to take it all away.

– Evaluation wasn't my line. I was a technician, by training. Maintenance work.

– Ah, the armourer, not the soldier. You just gave him the loaded gun. You didn't shoot anyone yourself. Well, who did?

There was no reply.

– Come on. We no longer keep secrets from each other. We're all friends now, you know.

He grinned, took out a cigarette and prepared to light it. The liaison officer stirred uneasily.

– I must inform you that smoking is not permitted in here.

– It is now.

A long silence ensued, into which the man from the ministry blew almost perfectly circular rings of smoke.

CHAPTER
II.II

A united national interest, as it was perceived in the then capital of Bonn, overrode these family squabbles. What project carried greater prestige, greater symbolic significance than an experiment in one of the most controversial questions of physics, locality versus non-locality, Einstein and Schrödinger versus Bohr, Heisenberg & Co. representing the so called Copenhagen school of thought – and carried out in Berlin, where quantum theory had its beginnings?

Although the twin-photon experiment originated under Suckfüll, the discredited director of our Institute in Berlin, and was continued in the name of his successor, Sichrovsky, it was Frank who was the man of the hour. It was Frank who had inveigled himself into the good graces of the men with power and money and secured us the services of both. It was Frank who persuaded them that the particular topography of Berlin, with its Wall breached but still in place, spoke strongly in favour of the large-scale experiment advocated by him, not only because it made spectacular science but because it was the best possible advertisement for the once divided and still ailing city which against everyone's expectations had now become one.

No question but that the man from the ministry with the backing of the Federal Government could declare non-smoking zones to be smoking areas if so he wished – that was the least of the special powers with which he had been invested. No matter how reluctant the telecommunications experts from the West were to share what they knew with their poor relations in the East, share was what they were going to have to do. And no matter how sceptical they were of the facilities they inspected at various sites in the former East Berlin – politics (with Frank nudging its elbow) had decided to confer the honour of Operations Centre on one of the few sites in the eastern sector with a name well known in the West, Potsdamer Platz.

In a former State Security listening post, in the basement of a house not five hundred metres from the cavernous puddle that had metamorphosed back into a pissoir, the Institute's long-distance twin-photon experiment would have its operational headquarters. The original plan had called for a photon track measuring a few dozen metres at most, to be installed in one of the Institute's basement laboratories. But Frank, the PR genius, outlined to the Ministry of Technology and Research a project to measure the correlation of entangled particles separated over a distance not merely of metres but of kilometres, and separated not just anywhere but with the most celebrated if no longer most impermeable man-made obstacle on the planet, the Berlin Wall, between them.

Creating a pair of entangled particles is itself no easy task. One way of doing so is to start with a single photon of ultraviolet radiation and pass it through a peculiar artificial mineral called a 'down-conversion crystal.' In our experiment, the crystal used consisted of potassium niobate. The crystal splits the photon in two, producing two new photons that continue on in somewhat different directions, and whose combined energy equals the energy of their parent photon.

Light from a laser diode passes through a dispersion prism and is focused into the down-conversion crystal. Behind the crystal, the pump is separated out by a filter while the passing down-converted photons are focused into one input port of a standard fibre coupler. In this way half of the pairs are split, exiting the twin-photon source at the tele-communications station on Potsdamer Platz by different output fibres.

One of the photons would be transmitted through 3.6 kilometres of pre-installed standard telecommunications optical fibre cable to an analyzer at a station at Alexander-platz. Using another installed fibre, the experimenters would send the other photon on a journey of 6.1 kilometres to a second analyzer at Tempelhof Airport. This was the set-up, a Franson-type experiment. The northbound signal passed through the heart of Berlin Mitte, entirely on the east side of the wall, while the southbound signal passed the Wall a couple of kilometres west of Checkpoint Charlie on its way to Tempelhof in the south.

For the technically-minded, to whom this jargon may mean something: the two analyzers consisted of all-fibre optical Michelson interferometers. An interferometer separates and then recombines beams of light by means of an arrangement of mirrors and 'beam splitters' — semi-opaque reflectors that randomly reflect some photons in one direction and transmit other photons in a different direction.

In which?

The choice was theirs.

Paraphrasing the above to make this complicated procedure more intelligible to the general reader: the experiment would start with a single ultraviolet photon, which was then split into two. One photon was sent one way, the other was sent another way, to identical analyzers, known as interferometers, at stations at Alexanderplatz and Tempelhof airport respectively.

Entering its own interferometer, the photon would have to make a random decision as to which of two paths it would travel through the device, a longer pathway to the right or a shorter one to the left. The 'decision' as to which path each of a pair of entangled photons would follow was therefore made by two particles at two points, Alexanderplatz and Tempelhof, separated on a north-south axis by the not negligible distance of seven kilometres.

Photodiodes would detect which path each of the two entangled photons had chosen and the scientists would look for a correlation between their pathways through the interferometer. In the Bohm-Aharanov type experiment considered by Bell[66], particles were correlated not by path selection but by orientation of spin, but the principle was the same.

If a statistically significant number of pathway correlations were found to have violated Bell's Inequality, it meant that in the instant one event had happened at Alexanderplatz, it had caused, or been caused by, or was in some inexplicable way synchronous with, another event at Tempelhof Airport, and this entanglement occurred by means of an operation unconstrained by the known limitations of classical physics covering time and space, forbidding anything to travel faster than the speed of light; meaning, in effect, that it would make no difference to the result of the experiment if Tempelhof and Alexanderplatz were relocated a billion light years apart.

CHAPTER
12

Pfrumpy noticed the first election poster on the wall of an old bomb site beside the tobacconist he stopped at in East Berlin. While Babaji went into the shop to buy cigarettes, Pfrumpy sat in the car looking at the poster on the bomb-site wall.

There was no picture, just words – the same four words Wilma had written down for him, licking the point of a drying felt-tip pen, in her round schoolgirl handwriting twenty years ago. The entry was under W, for Wilma, alongside a phone number in barely legible ink in the old pocketbook he always carried around with him, still did, for sentimental reasons.

When Babaji got back into the car he found Pfrumpy sitting in a trance. After a while Pfrumpy took the battered old address book out of his pocket, opened it at the page where Wilma had written four words, and handed it to Babaji. He pointed at these four words on the page. Then he pointed at the same four words on the poster on the bomb site wall.

Siebenundfünfzig Jahre sind genug.

Clearly this must have been a significant moment in the course of Pfrumpy's journey to Glienicker Bridge.

Pressed for a description of the state in which he found Pfrumpy when he got back into the car, Babaji could only say that he had seemed to be in a sort of daze.

Had Pfrumpy said anything?

Not that Babaji recalled. Pfrumpy had just asked him for a cigarette.[67]

To put this slogan into its context:–

During the fifty-seven years between the last free elections in 1933, held in East Germany in what was then the Weimar Republic before it succumbed to Hitler, and the elections held there after the Fall of the Wall in November 1989 but prior to national unification the following year, the country had experienced unbroken dictatorship under two successive regimes, the Nazis and the Communists.

If their history had also been, at least to some extent (and since quantum physics had done away with objective reality one felt bound to ask: how much?) their own doing, people had now, at any rate, had enough of those years with all the misery they had brought them, which was why they were putting up (a little warily, this kind of thing needed getting used to) election posters to say so. There was no indication who was responsible for the poster campaign. One wondered who was doing this, and also on whose behalf they were doing it; perhaps their own.

Who else was there to convince of the truth of the claim that fifty-seven years had been enough but those who had believed in it and been disappointed in their belief?

Once your attention has been drawn to something you have been in the habit of overlooking, you begin to see it as regularly as you failed to see it before. Babaji said he started noticing the Fifty-Seven Years Are Enough posters in places he frequently passed, like the fence around his local supermarket, where he had previously failed to notice them.

Babaji reported his poster findings to Pfrumpy, who showed an extraordinary interest in them.

It was in fact one particular poster Pfrumpy was looking for, one billboard, which must be located somewhere on a river, presumably on the Spree if the river was in Berlin.

They drove along both banks of the Spree, and where they couldn't drive they walked, following every sidearm and cul-de-sac, inlets into murky backwaters that ended in closed-down chemical plants, without success. But when, quite by chance, Pfrumpy drove out to Potsdam on his own one day and saw the billboard on the bank of the Havel as he was crossing Glienicker Bridge, he knew he must have found the site of which Wilma had dreamed.

That neither Pfrumpy nor Babaji showed any particular surprise at this late surfacing of a billboard Wilma had foreseen in a dream twenty years earlier, just dropped what they were doing and went off in search of it, tells us something about the nature of the miraculous, which is that for those receptive to it there is nothing particularly miraculous about it, it is part and parcel of the unexplained stuff making up quite a lot, perhaps even the bulk, of ordinary life.

CHAPTER
12.1

Wilma appears not to have been told that Pfrumpy and Babaji had been searching for the site of her dream, and neither she nor Babaji appears to have been told when Pfrumpy found it.[68] Whatever Pfrumpy's motives may have been on the approach to Glienicker Bridge, we begin to lose sight of them from this point on.

Pfrumpy kept a journal of sorts, in which he made jottings, undated, ungrammatical, often incoherent. Typically there would be a single word accompanied by an exclamation mark, the signature of the writer in a moved state of mind.

chair! blue!

These words were dashed off, sometimes quite illegibly. On page 10 of the pale blue notebook, manufactured with handmade paper and bearing the stamp of an upmarket stationery supplier in Wilmersdorf[69], about two-thirds of which remained unfilled, we find the single word *bridge*, without an exclamation mark and in a perfectly clear handwriting. Perhaps for this reason it manages to look subdued alongside all its rollicking companions.

Pfrumpy formed the letters of this word in a spirit clearly different from the spirit in which he formed the letters of other words. He has omitted to give it his signature tune. Where all the other words have been impetuously dashed off, this one looks as if it had been written in cold blood.

Bridge.[70]

What we surely *can* infer from Pfrumpy's silence about the bridge is that any motives traceable in Pfrumpy's conjectured world line on his approach to the bridge involved an element of secrecy. It is indeed this element of secrecy that suggests Pfrumpy may have *had* motives at all. The act of covering up reveals. The moment when we fail to detect a motive because it has been covered up may be when we first become aware of there being a motive to detect at all. There is something analogous to an Uncertainty Principle operating in human affairs as well.

Why is this an important issue?

It is important because it is the first evidence we have that human motives may have been involved in the events on Glienicker Bridge. It is the first evidence we have of an *intent*, prompting us to reconsider the use of the word *accident* when speaking of those events.

CHAPTER
13

Just imagine, I urged Peabody at our last meeting in his apartment in Montreal six months before he died, that view from the bridge. From the fragments we had been left we just had to try and put it together, to imagine was in the end our only way to collapse the wave function describing the probabilities that became actuality there.

Just imagine.

Pfrumpy might have sensed water beneath him. It rose up towards him from the ground, or perhaps it was the other way round, he was being lowered into it. He felt pressure on his skin, then a clammy coldness as his body was immersed. I shall drown, he said, struggling. At the end of a pair of elongated arms, holding him as he struggled, he saw far away on the other side of the room his mother's face and he heard her say, or some other woman say, for he was not sure of the sound of his mother's voice, that there was no help for it – a new-born child must first be given a bath before it could pass over into life.

Pfrumpy lay motionless when he awoke from this dream so as not to hasten its disintegration inside his head. Briefly he could hold the still unbroken dream in his conscious mind. He looked again curiously at his mother's face. Did she look like that? He could not remember having ever dreamed of her before. He could not remember her at all from the time when she lived – she had died when he was just a few years old.

This dream Pfrumpy would have dreamed on the morning of his fifty-seventh birthday. His birthday provided the pretext for the dream – the presence of water, the appearance of his mother, the post-natal bath, such images would flow naturally out of that pretext.[71]

Within moments of waking the dream crumbled and scattered.

— Well then, if that's the case...

There was light at the window. He could roughly tell the time by the murkiness of the light. It was around six o'clock.

He propped himself up on one elbow.

In the half-light of the room he saw that Wilma's bed was unslept in.

He crossed the room and stood at the open windows leading onto the balcony.

Pfrumpy stepped out.

He looked out over a lawn, a copse, stubble fields reaching to the horizon. Behind the copse, out of sight to the left, a village was hidden. He could see the church spire poking up behind the trees. The summer had burned. The crops had long been in. The stark burnt colour of the land was softened in the early September morning light. As the sun came up the birds that hung like thick black fruit in the rookery on the edge of the copse began to fidget and caw. A flock of them flew up out of the trees. On the path leading out of the copse he watched Wilma come walking slowly, swishing a stick through the grass.

In the past, this had been the landowner's house. Holm it had been called, after the family that built it. According to the agent of the co-operative from whom Pfrumpy had rented the place for the summer, the same family had been living here for a couple of hundred years, until the war ended, and they were driven out. Farm labourers living in the nearby hamlet that took its name from the landowner's house must have walked to work at this hour along the same path leading out of the copse from which Pfrumpy had just watched Wilma emerge.

She looked up and waved. Pfrumpy waved back.

The landowners had been living at Holm before the clock maker who was his great-grandfather was born, fifty kilometres away in Neu Cölln. They had still been here, watching labourers coming to work by the same path from the village across the fields, when Pfrumpy's great-grandfather had left Berlin for the New World.

Where were they now?

— Happy birthday!

Wilma blew him a kiss, crossed the terrace and entered the house.

The line of landowners once established here, the line of Pfrumpters that could be traced back to a clock-maker ancestor born in Neu Cölln whose people had left no record but had probably come from Poland — eventually the line was broken, traces kicked over, somewhere there was a gap, no heir, one way or another families petered out.

Wilma came up noiselessly behind him and ran her hand over the back of his head as she leaned over to kiss him.

— Happy birthday, my darling. You're up earlier than usual. Did the rooks wake you?

— Not this morning. It was a dream that woke me.

— What was the dream about?

Wilma perched on the cot by the house wall where Pfrumpy sometimes took his afternoon nap and drew her knees up under her chin.

She wore a faded blue cotton frock and a pair of sodden canvas shoes. Brambles along the path had scratched her wet shins, patterned her legs with a tracery of tiny specks of blood. Her arms and her throat were tanned a deep warm colour, made even deeper and warmer by the pale blue dress she had on. Thick black hair with twists of grey, bunched at the back in a large golden clasp, hung down over her shoulders onto her arms.

Wilma had turned forty that year.

Her figure had remained much as it had always been, not noticeably different from the seventeen year-old American-Indian girl Wilma had been when Pfrumpy first met her. Fine creases had puckered the corners of her mouth and put shadows around her eyes, but the cheeks were smooth, the forehead still unruffled. She was thinner than she used to be, more worn. Sitting there with her thin scratched legs drawn up under her chin, her knobbly elbows stuck out, she surprised Pfrumpy painfully with an aura of fragility he had not noticed about her before — an impression that was belied by the vitality of the strong black hair cascading over her shoulders.

— The dream was about being born. About my mother, and being given my first bath. Only . . .

— Only?

Pfrumpy was about to add that the sensation had been more like drowning, so in the end it might have been as much a dream about dying as about being born, but the vulnerability he sensed in Wilma held him back.

— I don't know, maybe it wasn't.

Pfrumpy lit a cigarette and passed it to Wilma.

— How about you? How was the dance?

— Well, as you see, I only just got home. The dance...

Wilma gave herself an odd little shake, took a drag and passed the cigarette back to Pfrumpy.

— The dance was all that a dance should be, everyone dancing, all the time, all night long.

— But when Frank and I left, the band were already packing their instruments.

— Right. And then, just after you and Frank left, Nikos showed up with a group of friends, Greeks, of course, musicians, who had been playing at someone's wedding and had dropped in at the restaurant for a bite to eat, and Nikos asked them if they would come over and play in the hall, and they did. They were wonderful.

— Did Nikos produce his mysterious bride?

— She's at home in the Lebanon, waiting for Nikos to come and fetch her. They still do things romantically over there. She'll be homesick here. It'll be a difficult start to the marriage for her in a strange country.

— When's the wedding?

— The end of October.

— We won't be here.

— We won't be here?

— The lease on the house will have run out by then. The house won't even be here any more.

— We can drive out from Berlin.

— Sure we can.

Pfrumpy knew that as well as Wilma did. But that wasn't what he had in mind when he said that they would be out of the house by the end of October. He had wanted to impress on Wilma that they would soon be *out of this house*, gone, the time it had lent them rooms to live in would all be used up. In the undertow of this peaceful summer morning, as of all the mornings preceding it, Pfrumpy felt the growing urgency, because coincidentally with Nick the Greek getting married their lease would expire, the developer who had bought the property from the co-operative would be moving in, tearing the place down to make room for a shopping centre – all in a rush it would have gone, their own six summer months here, with the demolition of the house all traces too of the summers of the family to whom this had been home for two hundred years.

Wilma must have picked up on what was passing through Pfrumpy's mind without him having to say it.

– You know what this has been reminding me of?

– Yes. It used to be like this when we closed up the cottage every summer and went back to the city in the fall.

– The last couple of years the prospect of that depressed me so much – I never told you this – I would almost have preferred not to go to the cottage at all.

– I felt the same.

Pfrumpy thought: so there's a contract covering a rental, there is cold weather on the way that will soon intervene, a roof that leaks, there are other less important matters to be attended to in Berlin – for no very good reason what seemed a perfectly liveable arrangement has to be broken up to make place for another. This is the law you have been given. You cannot stay as you are. You are always moving into a new state. Moving between one state and the next, comparisons that nag, even if you would have been content to stay as you are, you are the shuttlecock of that ceaseless unrest agitating between what was and will be, it is your destiny to be always caught between things remembered and things anticipated, missing the present all the while.

What he said was:

– If we hadn't come we wouldn't have to go. We could simplify our life.

– When we go to India we will. Which reminds me. I must go and talk to Babaji about lunch.

CHAPTER
13.1

A couple of weeks previously, Wilma had received from Friends of the Earth an invitation to run a photographers workshop for students in Calcutta. It was the first time she had been given professional recognition of this kind. Wilma was pleased, but she still hadn't replied, unable to make up her mind. The assignment was due to begin the following spring and would entail a stay of at least six months in India, one quarter, after all, of the two-year life expectancy — two years at the outside, perhaps much less — which she had been given by the doctor who had diagnosed Wilma's cancer.

For several days the doctor's verdict seemed to paralyse her ability to think.

True, she conceded, she might have lost weight, perhaps quite a lot. But she had not suffered any pain. There had been no other warning signs.

Not quite trusting the death sentence, not really believing it, Wilma had so far kept it to herself.

Wilma would have accepted the invitation without hesitation had she been sure that Pfrumpy and Frank would come with her. Pfrumpy was unenthusiastic but would go if that were the condition of her accepting, which he wanted her to do. Frank was committed to a research project for a telecommunications company, which it would be difficult but not impossible for him to get out of. Wilma didn't want to go without them. So when she spontaneously came out with that 'When we go to India' she took herself by surprise.

No such decision had yet been taken.

Wilma came out with the remark unthinkingly because the cancer had somehow slipped her mind.

Since yesterday evening she had not thought of the cancer once. During the last twelve hours, for the first time since Wilma had been told by the doctor, she had managed to forget about her secret. Afterwards this had worried Wilma.

– How is it possible to forget one's own death?

That 'When we go to India' was just what Wilma had been at pains to avoid.

If the project mattered to her that much she should go and do it on her own, but under these extreme circumstances she knew she was incapable of that. If she told Frank and Pfrumpy the truth of her situation, then naturally, that being her greatest, perhaps her last wish at all, they would agree to come along. But this would have been akin to blackmail and Wilma did not want that. The consequence was that Wilma kept her cancer to herself. And the consequence of keeping her cancer to herself was to pretend that she didn't want to take up the workshop assignment after all.

But she did want, and her want had asserted itself behind her back, as it were, with blank memory as an alibi who knew nothing abut a diagnosis of cancer, therewith removing the reason for her not wanting, so that in the end Wilma was able to blurt out her wish: 'When we go to India.'

There was a time when Pfrumpy would have picked up on that immediately, and a time before that when she needn't even have had to tell him what was going through her mind. She wouldn't have been able to keep her cancer a secret from him.

Moisture from the wet morning grass squeaking in her shoes, Wilma tiptoed back along the landing and looked into the first room she reached. Frank lay in bed on his back, his arms thrown back, his eyes shut, breathing lightly. Wilma had always liked to look at those she loved in the intimacy of their sleep, with a regret that she was excluded from it.

She wouldn't have had to tell Pfrumpy about last night's dance, either, which now she guessed she was going to have to do. She resented being forced to have these secrets from Pfrumpy. Pfrumpy was no longer reading her. Wilma felt let down.

Not today, however. It was Pfrumpy's birthday.

There were six for lunch, including Babaji's granddaughter and Frank's friend K., the philosophy graduate from the Institute who was writing a doctoral thesis about Frank's experiment. Wilma wondered about Frank and K., so different from Frank, a secretive, deep-sea creature who hovered on the fringe of Frank's light, feeding off Frank's openness and popularity. In return, K. offered Frank his adulation, which Frank in his inexhaustible vanity, always insecure, accepted as his due. K. stayed overnight, sleeping in the second bed in Frank's room, and Wilma reluctantly guessed that if Frank's admirer made any advances Frank would roll over on his back and accept these too.

The two of them drove back to Berlin with Babaji and his granddaughter the next morning, leaving Wilma and Pfrumpy on their own in the house.

It might naturally have been expected that the addition of Frank to the household would have had an impact on its members, required some kind of adjustment to their lives. But Babaji, our sole surviving witness, speaks of a household accord between Wilma and Pfrumpy that was not noticeably affected by Frank's arrival. It seems, if anything, to have deepened into a still stronger sense of cohesion among the inmates of the house, only that now, with the inclusion of Frank, it was based on a tripartite equilibrium.

In Babaji's practically minded view, this balance was guaranteed by the optimal amount of space available to each of them. Neither too much nor too little, a degree of distance from one another appears to have been the condition of their closeness.

In terms of distance from the large common room taking up most of the ground floor, Pfrumpy up in the garret lived at the furthest remove and occupied the least space. The so-called garret was in fact an ornamental Wilhelminian tower. This was Pfrumpy's room. It led onto a tiny roof terrace, not more than a few square metres, lined with boxed geraniums whose winter hardiness surprised the secretaries of the Bleibtreu insurance office opposite no less than Pfrumpy's resilience when sitting out in the cold with no clothes on.

From the garret Pfrumpy climbed down a steep narrow staircase to the third floor. Here he breakfasted, or, depending on the time of day, lunched with Wilma in an alcove overlooking the corner of the street where it met with the Kurfürstendamm.

Across the passage from the alcove there was a library where Babaji would usually be at work by the time Pfrumpy came down in the mornings. The shelves on the walls housed a lot of bound Tibetan manuscripts, long narrow books about the size of a cigarette carton, as well as a collection of other books in Chinese, Khotanese, Pali and Sanskrit.

Adjacent to the alcove was a pantry where Wilma or Pfrumpy could fix themselves a meal when they didn't want to bother Babaji. The pantry led through to a large bare-floorboarded room that Wilma had converted into her studio. Beyond that lay her bedroom and bathroom.

On the floor below were two spare rooms, or rather suites, one of them permanently occupied by Frank ever since Wilma had found him living in a tent on Potsdamer Platz and taken him in.

These had been the original master bedrooms. They opened onto a sort of salon in the middle, which Frank had adopted as his study. The guests in Pfrumpy's house lived in much grander style than their hosts. Frank certainly did, for a couple of years. Wilma had made her tiny bedroom out of a former walk-in closet. Pfrumpy up in his tower slept on the floor, a habit he had acquired in Ladakh and retained ever since.

Babaji, his personal needs and his needs as quartermaster of the house, commanded the ground floor, his pantry, his kitchen, the dining-room and a large common living-room where everyone would converge late in the evening after dinner.

Perhaps there was something to Babaji's theory about an 'optimal amount of space.' But Frank's insertion into this living space without upsetting it can only have been possible given some vacancy for Frank to fill; and Babaji, as we have seen, identified that vacancy with Wilma's need for someone she could have around her in what she felt to be her aloneness.

CHAPTER
14.1

A few weeks after he came to the house Frank woke up one morning to find Pfrumpy sitting on the end of his bed. It had been an unusually warm night for the time of year. Frank had uncovered himself in his sleep. Pfrumpy looked down on Frank with smiling eyes, even the creases at the corners, it seemed to Frank, somehow tinged with the traces of a not quite fathomable smile. Pfrumpy waited until Frank was fully awake before he began to speak [72].

– Frank, now that you are here. We should talk about Wilma. Wilma is a woman with, well. What?

Frank, who had only just woken up, was not yet prepared to deal with such a question.

– I'm nor sure I know what you're driving at. Tell me, Pfrumpy.

– More love in her than there are people in her life she has been able to give it to. Love as a gift. Is this some kind of mystery? Is the nature of love properly understood?

Pfrumpy waited, his head cocked, as if listening for something which, should it be audible, would be much further away than Frank's answer.

– There are always at least two here. The receiver must have a gift for receiving, don't you think, hardly less than the giver's gift of giving. Certainly I alone am not enough for Wilma to love. There is more in her to give than there is in me to receive. Had there been children for her to love, and to our regret there have not, they wouldn't in the end have been enough, either. Would she have done better to adopt?

– If she would have, she would.

– Maybe she would. She waited because she wanted her own.

Perhaps she waited too long, and in the meantime it is too late. She feels the cold at her back. She still continues to need these now ghostly children. For the love that Wilma has to give, Frank, is a gift, which can only be received in the unselfconscious way that children have. Needy recipients, whose greedy taking of gifts corresponds perfectly to Wilma's greed to give them. Without thanks or evasions or the notion that they have to give something back in return, or any feeling beyond the certainty that they are rightful receivers. They soak up whatever is given as their due. It becomes part of them and they grow out of this base. You may think you can recognise here, I mean, can you? – a selfishness on the part of the giver no less than there is on the receiver's. The giver demands the allegiance of the receiver, such that one may wonder: is the gift of love not also an imposition, which can cause resentment on the part of the person receiving it? Is it also an exercise of power over the receiver? Is the giving contingent upon the payment of a tribute, something exacted by the giver from the receiver, providing grounds for justifying the giver's giving nature, the giver's existence as such?

Pfrumpy got up, towering, somewhat intimidating, Frank felt, over the bed.

– Wilma is bound, one might even say enslaved by a need to do something for someone, to take their loss upon herself, to put herself in their shoes, to feel for them. Almost as if she had to make amends for something – and were it only for us all being in the sometimes desperate human condition we are. This is love in the most chaste of its selfless forms, taking upon itself the pain of the world, just that, and those in whom this gift is to be found are the natural nobility of the world. They are the torch-bearers for all the rest of us. They connect things that would otherwise remain without connection. So you must treat Wilma with more concern than you would ever treat yourself, Frank. It will make you a better person. It will benefit you, but even more it will benefit her. So whatever she has to give, Frank, *whatever*, you must receive. Receiving becomes your responsibility, Frank.

Pfrumpy walked to the door, turned and looked back at him.

– Wilma's life is in your hands, Frank.

CHAPTER
14.2

But Frank didn't know what to make of all this. Pfrumpy's unexpected parting shot about having Wilma's life in his hands — Frank was completely baffled.

We must talk, Pfrumpy had said to him at the outset. But then there had been no more 'we' about it. Pfrumpy had delivered a prepared speech to Frank, not engaged in a conversation with him, walking out of the room once he had delivered that parting shot before Frank was able to collect his wits. Frank couldn't get a word in edgeways, and he wasn't used to that.

Pfrumpy's smile-creased eyes were unfathomable.[73] Frank sensed that when the occasion arose there could also be something about Pfrumpy that made you feel extremely uncomfortable.

He thought he would just ignore what Pfrumpy had said, but he was underrating Pfrumpy's persuasiveness. To his irritation, Frank found himself unable to shake off the suggestion that he had somehow taken on a responsibility for Wilma. Like a ditty, it followed him around. *Wilma's life is in your hands* — what a peculiar thing to say, and for Frank to feel bound to obey.

Wilma dissolved and reintegrated as a tune in Frank's head that wouldn't go away. The tune accompanied him whatever he was doing and wherever he went.

What was the tune and how had it got into his head? Had Wilma put it there? Or Pfrumpy?

Frank wondered.

On Sichrovsky's assignment, Frank was now trekking back and

forth several times a day between Potsdamer Platz, Alexanderplatz and Tempelhof Airport, co-ordinating technical functions at the three sites of the twin-photon experiment, and found he was always carrying Wilma around with him, a tune he had on the brain. Wilma was in some sense always there.

Her gift was no longer the kind of remote viewing she had done as a student for the experiments in Montreal, just an extended reach of her ordinary perceptions, as if Wilma could glance across at Frank on the other side of the city. She often knew where Frank had been during the day without him having to tell her. In the same way she glanced up and saw Frank, she checked on Pfrumpy too, up in his tower room, driving around town or closeted with Babaji, poring over their manuscripts in the library across the passage from the studio dark room where Wilma spent an hour or two every day. This was when the unprompted internal imaging came most easily to her mind, whether the person was in the house or on the other side of town. Distance had nothing to do with it.

Much to his surprise, Frank discovered he had ceased to be alone. There was somebody else around. It was as if he now weighed all his decisions and shared all his perceptions with someone who was always around, listening in and looking on.

This was at the same time a heart-warming and a deeply shocking discovery.

Frank wondered if the refrain in his head was like some kind of a homing device for Wilma. A roving wavelength, arriving wherever the ditty was, wherever she could be received – something like that? Was the tune his or hers?

He wondered about a double sense in Pfrumpy's words when he told Frank that 'receiving' had become his responsibility.

It gradually dawned on Frank what Pfrumpy might have meant by the giver's gift imposing an obligation on the receiver. He was bound to accept the gift. The gift came with strings attached, like Wilma's life being in his hands, and Frank wasn't sure he wanted all that involved. He wasn't sure he could manage it. But it seemed he had no choice in the matter. Did Wilma?

— No.

— We have no choice in the matter?

— I think it works differently, Frank.

— How does it work?

— I don't think we choose. I think we're chosen.

— By what?

— By what attracts us. You may be standing waiting somewhere, nowhere in particular. I don't know. Someone or something comes along, and nowhere in particular becomes a destination at which you find you have arrived. The things that matter in your life happen without your choosing them. You don't choose them. They happen to you. These are not things over which you have control. Choosing is just the appearance, an illusion, the terms under which we find acceptable things that are not of our choosing and may not really be acceptable to us at all.

— For what is after all, — at any rate the way *you* describe it, Wilma — just a *lack* of something, you make it sound like it was a pretty big deal . . . I don't know.

Under the languorous effect of Wilma's beautiful mezzo voice, besieged by the deep quality of her voice, Frank had difficulty finding faults, which he otherwise had no difficulty doing, with what the voice was saying.

— So was that what happened at Potsdamer Platz? Is that what you're saying?

— Mmm.

Wilma snuggled up beside him and nuzzled Frank's neck. He put his arms round her.

— Does Pfrumpy know you're down here with me?

— He's down here with us.

— Where?

Frank raised his head and looked anxiously through the open door into the salon, half expecting to see Pfrumpy sitting at the Louis XV escritoire or reclining on the yellow chaise longue. Wilma laughed.

CHAPTER
14.21

Frank's suppressed bisexual nature, the source of so many ambivalent leanings in him, was only allowed to come into its own after he went to live with Wilma and Pfrumpy.

Until then he had felt himself a misfit, not wholly comfortable either with men or with women. What until then he had felt as a defect, his physical incompleteness, his falling short of a fully achieved masculinity, was perceived by Wilma, however, as something beautiful. What he wanted to hide she wanted him to show, and what she showed him was a revelation — that something shameful in his own eyes could become an object of love in hers.

No doubt this made it possible for Frank to begin to talk about things he had previously kept to himself. From a remark he once made to me it seemed that in infancy he had suffered some kind of illness, which had later inhibited his sexual development.

On another occasion he spoke of a condition that was 'congenital', which, whether or not Frank meant it intentionally, struck me as a rather witty description of his bisexuality.

Shaking his long mane of hair and laughing, often in the wake of some provocative remark he had made, Frank had a way of keeping one in two minds that was charming, almost flirtatious. Perhaps the secret of charm, whether in men or in women, has a feminine base in its capacity to mediate. This was certainly the case with Frank. He released a physical flow that was palpable around any room he was in. Lubricated, people flowed with it.

There was apparently an undertow to this that went deeper, as can be inferred from a mysterious passage excerpted by Pfrumpy in his book of commonplaces.[74]

'...a secret, namely, that within the Unconscious the third (term) is getting prepared and is already beginning to neutralise the energy of the tension between two opposites; i.e. *the illusion that opposites really are opposites fades, and with it the axioms of symmetry.* This process is typically 'eastern', for the teaching of *mukti* (liberation) as of *tao* means overcoming opposites in the actual world (*samsara*) and gaining insight into the illusion (*maya*) behind it.'[75]

Why was this 'a secret'? What was the nature of 'the third' within the Unconscious? What did 'getting prepared' mean?

Maybe 'the third' was in some way connected with Pfrumpy's remark to Frank during their bedside conversation that 'there are always at least two here'. Three, then. Perhaps more. But the quotation remains mysterious.

On the one side there was Wilma, feminine in her mediating function that went far beyond the usual meaning of these words. On the other side there was Pfrumpy, self-sufficient, dutiful, rock-solid but without obvious warmth, combative rather than collaborative. Did these two constitute a pair of opposites in Pfrumpy's mind?

How did Frank fit in here?

CHAPTER
14.211

Hardly ever would one observe bodily contact between Wilma and Pfrumpy. One noticed all the more the frequency of physical exchanges between Pfrumpy and Frank, a kind of Middle Eastern intimacy, something not really European at all, a hand touching an arm, an arm lingering around a shoulder. A curious, even rather absurd impression formed in my mind, not so much of two people in physical contact with one another, really more like a single organism, some sort of many-branched sea plant, wavy and ticklish, interlocking tendrils from time to time as if keeping track of itself.

In some circles in Berlin, which rather prided themselves on the city's liberal traditions, it was taken for granted that a good-looking young man and a wealthy older man who advertised their mutual affection in this way would be sexual partners as well. The fact that Frank and Pfrumpy were seen together at a gay club in Pankow, to which they were introduced by Sichrovsky, then still a closet homosexual (it had not even got into his file), certainly helped to fuel those rumours. Sichrovsky got drunk one evening and made a pass at Frank in Pfrumpy's presence. When refused, Sichrovsky spitefully and somewhat anachronistically (we had long since left the class struggle behind us) called him a capitalist slut who peddled his arse to the rich.

It was a disgraceful scene.

Frank and Pfrumpy never went back. Sichrovsky apologised. But Frank's professional relations with the Institute director on the joint project they were working on were impaired for the remainder of the project's term of life.

Since it is the nature of gossip to pry out secrets, there's an irresistible tendency among gossip-prone people to make the most of their secrets by assuming the worst. This is the coinage in which gossip is traded, the worth accorded the gossip. The damage is in the intent. The damage is already being done before the secret is out.

All this was perfectly familiar to us in East Berlin. Post-Wall gossip seemed child's play to us. We had known the serious version. It was gossip that our former ministry of state security had collected and kept in its files, gossip that killed people or put them behind bars, maimed their lives.

There was a willingness, a great exertion of willingness, to overlook a straightforward truth about Frank and Pfrumpy because in the world of rumourmongers simplicity and truth are counter-productive qualities. Rumours are never kind or give anyone the benefit of the doubt. There must always be something to nothing. Yet the simple truth was that Frank and Pfrumpy just enjoyed each other's company.

In academic circles, gossip mongering can come in laborious, if not to say laboured forms. On the blackboard of the Institute someone left a caricature of Frank as the smooth-haunched heifer Europa being mounted by a snorting North American Indian bull, complete with swinging bollocks and feathered head-dress, done in coloured chalks with considerable graphic talent, even humour, it has to be said. It wouldn't have been perpetrated by Sichrovsky himself (he didn't have the sense of humour, let alone the talent), but he might well have put someone up to it.

The proof of 'innocence', in the end, was the lack of proof of anything to the contrary, the lack of any hints in the mass of private papers left behind by Wilma and Pfrumpy – neither of whom had any problems being candid in their self-dealings – regarding any sort of sexual activity in which Frank and Pfrumpy might have been engaged.

Or are we perhaps overlooking their participation in some sort of threesome with Wilma?

CHAPTER
14.212

In one of Wilma's weekly picture logs there is a photo of a very tall conical shape taking up all the space between the floor and the high ceiling, four metres at least, of one of those high Berlin rooms. Background details identify it as the connecting room between the two bedrooms on the second floor where Frank lived. The photo includes the right foot of the photographer, lying in bed on her back and shooting the picture down over her body, and a left foot beside it, so far not identified with forensic certainty, but presumably Pfrumpy's.[76]

The photo log alongside reads: 'We all spent the morning in bed and laughed a lot at Frank being a ghost.'

Frank must be the conical shape standing on the Louis XVI dresser, one corner of which peeps out, swathed in the 4-metre long white curtains Wilma took down and replaced with blue ones, his head and shoulders entirely swallowed up inside the giant lampshade Wilma commissioned from the designer Stefan Wewerka.

Babaji testifies that the three of them did a lot of 'fooling around.'

When Lawrence Peabody asked Babaji outright: What sort of fooling around? Just pretending to be a ghost and stuff like that? Adding snidely: or engaging in the more usual sort of adult activities that go on in Sunday morning bedrooms? – the old man, visibly shocked, gently shook his head.

What did that shaking of the head signify?

To me much later, long after Peabody had gone, Babaji said: 'The three of them, after Frank came, you know, they were often like children, they really just enjoyed playing with each other, do you know?'

To Babaji, the kind of prying Peabody did into the private lives of his clients, even if it was done for professional reasons, was deeply distasteful, he disliked intensely the prurience he sensed behind such inquiries, for whatever reason they might be undertaken. It offended the innocence of Babaji's sensibility, grounded though it was in sensually flesh-loving traditions of Hinduism that would naturally have shaped whatever views the celibate Babaji held on sex, and which would have incorporated such sensuality as part of Babaji's 'innocence' without any burden of contradiction. Which was to say that what Babaji called 'just playing with each other' might have been called something different by the Peabodies of this world.

The important point easily overlooked in this discussion is Babaji's impression of three adults playing like children only *after* Frank's arrival. Whatever bodies are or are not doing in bed on Sunday morning is secondary to the consideration of the *light-heartedness* with which it is being done. This is what Frank brought into Wilma's and Pfrumpy's house, into their lives, a quality that seems to have become overgrown and disappeared in the increasing seriousness of the twenty years the couple had spent together; with all the baggage accumulated en route piling up, beginning to take up more room than the route itself, the coming to terms with things as they are, the unremarkable erosion, perhaps the sadder for being unremarkable, of hopes of some kind of change for some kind of better, in the end of any change at all – cumulatively those reluctant but overwhelming insights which belong to the biography of all marriages.

Beyond that, what goes on at the heart of a marriage may not really be knowable, least of all to those who are the heart of it themselves. It is not the concern of those who are outside. That said, there remains one intimate question that still needs to be addressed.

CHAPTER
14.3

Two or three times I heard from Frank an allusion to the story of Orpheus and Eurydice. There was a film of the story, set in Rio de Janeiro during the time of carnival, which Frank took me to see at a cinema in West Berlin[77]. But the film running in Frank's head was another one. In Frank's version, it was Orpheus who had gone down into the nether kingdom of the dead, playing his harp to himself by way of whistling in the dark, Eurydice who had followed and successfully brought him back to life in the upper world. Eurydice was a name by which Frank sometimes called Wilma.

The Orpheus-Eurydice story in this amended version served Frank and Wilma as a mirror in which they found an image of themselves. There was first of all the question: why did Orpheus go down into the nether world if not to fetch back Eurydice? Because he was doomed to go down on his own. This 'doom', as it was felt to be by Frank, can only be understood, as Wilma did, by putting herself in Frank's shoes and walking him all the way down to ground zero, the last of those twenty-six subterranean levels beneath Tempelhof Airport. There among piles of corroding metal against which she got Frank to pose naked he revealed to her his secret, began, since he could not tell it to her straight, to confess it to her in sexual allegories, a familiar but twisted story about an Orpheus who had to play his harp to himself because he was unable to play it for any woman.

Whether Frank became able to play it for Wilma and thus felt himself brought back to life, as their Orpheus was by Eurydice, is thus really a question about whether she substituted her helping hand for his, whether she released Frank from the self-playing solipsism of masturbation and brought him over into the practice of sex as a union consummated by two people. Judging from the striking change that came over Frank after his paths crossed Wilma's at Potsdamer Platz, his comment to Babaji [78] on the first morning he woke up in Wilma's house, his admission to me of the 'relief' he felt afterwards, it seems very probable that something like that must have been the case.

But we have to go on and ask: beyond Frank being masturbated by Wilma, was he capable of an erection sufficient to penetrate a woman and ejaculate inside her vagina, and if so, with what results beyond a sensation of pleasure?

Almost ten years would pass before I was given a qualified answer to this question. The question only really posed itself in this very explicit form as a result of my visit to Montreal to talk to Lawrence Peabody in the late 1990s — just six months, it turned out, before Pea died. Had I waited a little longer I would not have been able to talk to him and Pea would have taken his information to the grave.

Pea's information bore primarily upon Pfrumpy, the terms of his will, the settlements on behalf of a very considerable number of institutions and individuals named in the will as legatees. After Pfrumpy's death, it took Pea most of his own remaining life to execute all the provisions of that unusually complex testament. Because ramifications arising from Pea's information were at least in theory possible, and might have rampaged as a legal nightmare, and because above and beyond the requirements of his job Pea was by nature an extremely cautious and secretive man, he withheld that information until the very end.

The information had a direct bearing on the question: did Pfrumpy and his wife continue to have sex with each other up until the time of their death in the fall of 1992? Pea could not of course ask either of the parties concerned, as both of them were dead. The one person who might have been able to shed light on the matter was Babaji. But Babaji had been offended by Pea's cynicism in that question about the precise nature of the 'fooling around' in Sunday beds, in Frank's, come to that, which might have been what worried Pea, his mind on the consequences of Wilma's producing an illegitimate heir, most of all. Babaji clammed up, not a word more was to be got out of him.

In my own interviews with Pfrumpy, however, at least a year after he had resumed the yoga practice of $gTum$-mo[79], I incidentally learned from him that $gTum$-mo practice was incompatible with having sex. A serious practitioner had to choose one or the other, to continue with both was 'infeasible' – it seemed to me a curious choice of word, which was probably why I remembered it. Pfrumpy was a very serious practitioner, without doubt. This offers no unassailable proof that for as long as he was in Berlin Pfrumpy did not have sexual relations with his wife, but it comes very close to it, and here lies the problem.

When I returned from Montreal, I went to see the pathologist who had conducted autopsies on all three bodies recovered from the river seven years previously. In the opinion of the pathologist, the atrophied condition of Frank's genitals would have made normal intercourse impossible. His penis was too small and would in any case have been unable to sustain an erection allowing him to penetrate and inseminate a woman, even assuming seed production to have been possible, in the ordinary way.

I did not of course raise with the pathologist my own doubts about Pfrumpy's sexual capacities during the three years prior to his death, for the reach of all that didn't concern him. I was thus left on my own with all these obstinate facts, obliged somehow to reach my own conclusions from the information I had only recently been given by Peabody and which the pathologist now confirmed; namely, that in the womb of the dead woman he had found a nut-sized embryo indicating that Wilma must have been in about the sixth week of pregnancy; a pregnancy, the pathologist added, which may not have been known to the deceased herself at the time of her death.

CHAPTER
15

Towards the end of the last summer they spent at Holm – and we did not need to conjecture this, as I told Peabody in Montreal, we knew it for a fact – there was a folk music festival in the village that went on for several days. Pfrumpy and Wilma went every night to the village hall to hear groups play – Greeks, Turks, Sephardic Jews from Morocco – to an audience of usually not more than fifty or sixty people. Nikos had organised and Pfrumpy sponsored the event in order to publicise the restaurant Nikos had opened in the village. Each night it was never more than a handful of people who made the journey out from Berlin. After the concerts there was dancing that went on all night, but Pfrumpy had never cared much for dancing. He usually went home around midnight and left Wilma to it.

Four nights in succession Wilma stayed out until dawn, and with a growing numbness of heart, long aware of something hidden in Wilma that seemed, in the hazy picture he had been able to form of it, to be a crack of some kind, Pfrumpy would watch from the balcony of the house as she came down the path that led out of the copse, swishing a stick through the dew-soaked grass, the rooks flying up out of the trees and cawing when she passed.

Wilma sat with her knees drawn up under her chin and said to Pfrumpy beside her:

– I was out last night in the fields, you know, actually the last couple of nights, with a man I met at the village dance. One of the musicians. One of those casual affairs. I don't really know how it happened. I'm sorry. There was that wonderful music they played. It took me away, and

I forgot everything. Just for a while I was able to – escape.

Pfrumpy said nothing, waiting for Wilma to go on.

She then told him about her cancer.

– Now I don't want to go to India any more. Now I don't want to change anything. I want everything to go on quite normally just as it is. I want us to go back to our house in Berlin and live there happily together for as long as it takes.

Wilma laid her head on Pfrumpy's shoulder and began to cry.

– I want to stay at home. I don't want to have to escape anywhere again. Please don't let me go. Please don't send me away.

Pfrumpy put his arms round her, touching the top of her head with his lips, sniffing the early morning scent of her hair, and could feel the crack in his heart that was her own.

– I think the bird just flew back. This time the bird is here to stay.

Pfrumpy had never slept much, and during their last summer at Holm one can imagine (as I said to Peabody) that Wilma would have joined him in that sleepless place in the dip of the night just before daybreak. They lay talking about other places they had been together and the things they had done, long after it had grown light. Gently Pfrumpy steered her along these paths, so that Wilma wouldn't notice she was being led. Bringing to mind memories Pfrumpy knew gave her pleasure, Wilma would begin to feel quiet again and eventually go back to sleep.

The weather held. On perfect late summer days Wilma would play the game she had played as a child, holding a finger up to the sun and seeing the finger become transparent, as though a light went on inside her skin.

At such moments she could be almost happy.

They kept quiet at Holm and learned to read the lie of the land. Careful not to disturb, they walked on tiptoe through flawless days, to Pfrumpy as brittle as glass, went for cycle rides and swam in the river, Wilma whistling softly to herself on their way home in the dark.

Everything held, as if it had always been like this and always would.

Wilma began to feel secure.

– Perhaps if we keep quiet it will just go away. What do you think? Maybe they made a mistake and it won't happen after all.

– Maybe.

– But if it does, what will become of you, Pfrumpy? What will Frank do?

Here lay for Pfrumpy the greatest mystery – that Wilma's dream of precognition, dreamed the night before they had first met in his just dead father's house, would now somehow come to pass, twenty-three years later, in connection with the lease on this other house that was now about to expire. What the dream had foreseen running out was not the span of Wilma's forty years of life, however. The numbers had very particularly referred to his. It was not Wilma whose lease would be running out. It was Pfrumpy.

Fifty-seven years would be enough.

Turning it over and over in his mind in the two decades since, wondering what the dream meant, Pfrumpy had felt himself drawn into expecting that, for whatever reason, when he reached the age of fifty-seven his life would, in some way which Wilma had been able to divine, *be enough*.

Perhaps the dream did not mean that, but for better or worse this was the interpretation to which Pfrumpy had become resigned.

During the couple of years since he discovered the corroboratory billboard, reading on it, in enormous letters, the exact same words of the judgement Wilma had passed and written down at the time in his address book, the proof in his hand, it had penetrated into his bones, become his death sentence.

And now Wilma seemed to be telling him the prediction concerned her own death, not his. Had she forgotten? Had she made a mistake? Even when she iced onto the cake his fifty-seventh birthday greetings, stuck the candles on top and counted them one by one, there was still no glimmer of recollection, in all innocence Wilma could still ask 'What will become of you, Pfrumpy?' – although it was Wilma herself who had delivered the prediction he had been waiting all those years to see fulfilled.

What did it mean?

When the weather broke, dismantling the summer, they packed their bags, closed up the house and drove back to Berlin.

Watching the vast flat land recede slowly in the rear mirror, it seemed to Pfrumpy he was watching themselves dwindling into the distance and vanishing under the horizon. As they approached Glienicker Bridge, and his shining with it rose to an audible humming in his ears, the answer presented itself of its own accord. The words Wilma had dreamed meant that the lease would expire on the house Pfrumpy had lived in on the same day that Nick the Greek got married and Wilma died. It meant that on that day *he died her death*, the one was entangled inseparably with the other, for what was her death unless a part of his life, his life unless a part of her death?

CHAPTER
16

Thanks to the falling out between Frank and Sichrovsky, made worse by Sichrovsky's belief he could manage such matters just as well himself, the press conference at which the results of the Twin Photon Experiment were announced attracted little attention outside Berlin, or even just East Berlin, according to our detractors (of whom there were many) in the west. Frank would have arranged a reception at the best hotel in town and had the event televised, making sure the international press was there to cover it.

Sichrovsky, still very much a child of the hermetic state that had since passed into oblivion, did his best to keep it a secret. He called the press conference at the 'barracks', as they were internally known, on a cold March morning in an unheated lecture hall. No refreshments were offered to the handful of local journalists and a couple of science correspondents representing national newspapers.

In his flat, rather high-pitched voice Sichrovsky read a statement overburdened with statistics and technical jargon. What finally buried the presentation was a defective microphone in the hall, making sure that the largely unintelligible remained largely inaudible, too. Whatever escaped the lecture hall had soon disappeared in a paragraph somewhere deep inside a newspaper. The 'press conference' was a total fiasco.

But the gist of the Institute's remarkable experiment could have been put tersely and sensationally.

All around us in the world a mysterious correlation of events was taking place, of one thing knowing what another was doing however far away it was and apparently exchanging that knowledge a million times faster than the speed of light; simultaneously, in effect. This should have made world headlines, but it didn't, not anywhere outside the trade press, as I recall.[80]

As it was, the press conference produced an anti-climax that left us with a feeling of flatness and a bitter aftertaste in our mouths. If Frank, Wilma and Pfrumpy hadn't hosted the 'Twin-photon Luncheon' (Frank) that day the project team would have gone home feeling very depressed. Sichrovsky excused himself, to everyone's relief, as he had to leave immediately for Leipzig and deliver in person an address to physicists there on the results we had obtained in Berlin. It wasn't physics that took Sichrovsky to Leipzig. It was the settling of old scores with the faculty there.

It was my first visit to Pfrumpy's house. Nine of us sat down to lunch at three o'clock in the afternoon, by which time we were well-lubricated. The group included Jens, who was Sichrovsky's second-in-command at the Institute, a PhD. student by the name of Sommerfeld (no relation to the eminent quantum physicist), the project engineer Schmidt, the science correspondent of the FAZ and Professor Q., a visiting American physicist currently working at Humboldt whom none of us had ever met before. Babaji set huge bowls of curry and rice on the table and left us to help ourselves.

Frank, as usual, held forth. Partly out of courtesy to our hosts, partly to accommodate the American who knew no German, the conversation was held largely in English. If I had thought the courtesy to our hosts was a formality, as the conversation might well be expected to leave non-specialists stranded whatever language it was held in, I was mistaken in Pfrumpy's case. I didn't know at the time that he had trained as a chemist. Whatever Pfrumpy had learned as a student from the work of Delbrück and others who had raised the foundations of modern chemistry on quantum physics, he had evidently not forgotten it. Pfrumpy sat at one end of the table with a look of amusement on his face as he listened to Frank holding forth at the other.

Frank rapidly cleared the ground of experimental debris – technical weaknesses in the methodology, which would have to be improved on next time – to move on to the obvious question, the small print, as it were, of the world headline.

– So what's the trick? How does it work?

The American professor answered promptly.

– Subluminal communication, I continue to believe, even if that opinion may not be popular here, between the components of our measuring apparatus. OK, it was a very impressive series you ran. But close the detection loopholes – and one of these days we will – and you'll find locality upheld, no spooky action at a distance, game and set to Einstein.

Jens objected.

– I don't think so. We are refining and refining the apparatus and getting finer and finer results the more the detection loopholes are closed – an average of fifteen coincidences every two seconds this last time, OK, meaning 80% visibility. The finer the grain of the results, the more they work against the assumption of locality. Just look at the evidence of the research done during the last twenty years by Freedman, Clauser, Horne, Shimony and Holt, Aspect, Dalibard, Sichrovsky et al – that's us, by the way, in case you didn't know –

Jens laughed.

– There's an unmistakable trend here, and it's going fast in the other direction. The main obstacle to further progress is really that nonlocality makes a lot of physicists nervous.

– Doesn't it make *you* nervous?

Frank flapped his arms vigorously, as if to clear the smoke from the table. The amused look on Pfrumpy's face broadened into a big smile. You could watch him enjoying Frank.

– Let us assume the loopholes are closed by ever more conclusive techniques, changing the polarizer angles in flight, and so on. These ever more refined experiments continue to give evidence of non-classical correlations. There *is* a simultaneity of events occurring separated in space, but in another sense inseparable. The local, deterministic explanation, which derives the correlations from a common cause, some pre-prepared features embedded in the parent particle, eventually has to be discarded, even by its most ardent champions, such as our guest Professor Q. What is your next move, Professor?

The American hesitated for a few seconds.

– Just an idea.

He held up a warning hand.

– All your measuring equipment is stationary, fixed, right? What if you introduced relativity into the experimental set-up, by having both sets of equipment in motion relative to each other. I don't know quite how...but in theory, at any rate, it should be possible to create a situation in which according to the measuring equipment at Tempelhof the incoming photon there is analysed before the arrival of its twin at Alexanderplatz. But according to the equipment at Alexanderplatz, thanks to relativity, it's the other way round, the photon *there* thinks *it* arrived first, the twin at Tempelhof second . . . so both photons arrive first, or putting it another way, neither arrives second, and so the response of neither can be said to be *dependent* on the other. You see? In such a case, no communication takes place, there *is* no exchange of information, and accordingly I wouldn't expect to find any correlations between the particles.

He glanced at his watch and immediately jumped to his feet.

– Half past five! My *gosh* . . . I'm afraid I . . . oh dear . . . I had no idea how late it already was . . .

The abrupt departure of the American provided the pretext for the science correspondent and the engineer, neither of whom I could recall having put in a word all afternoon, to take their leave as well. It was a smaller group that moved over into the lounge but perhaps for that reason a more comfortable one, which didn't break up until early the next morning[81].

CHAPTER
16.1

With the departure of Q. and Co. we talked about other things. The conversation had been wandering around amiably enough, from this to that and back again, for the past hour or two when Pfrumpy came and sat down heavily beside Jens with an audible explosion of the sofa springs.

– Why did you say to Q. that nonlocality made physicists nervous?

– They don't know what to do with it. It upsets the world they are familiar with.

– I seem to remember -

Pfrumpy got up again, took a book down from the shelf behind him and began leafing through it.

– When you run out of things you know, you must imagine them . . . . as Bohm does, for instance.

– Who?

– David Bohm.

– Oh.

– Bohm has some interesting suggestions to make about non-locality.

Intrigued that Pfrumpy had a book of Bohm's in the house, whom I greatly admired, I got up from the sofa where Wilma was having a conversation with Frank and Babaji that didn't interest me and went over to Pfrumpy to see which of Bohm's books it was. It was a rather battered copy, heavily annotated with underlinings and scrawlings in a tiny handwriting, Pfrumpy's, it turned out, of Bohm's extraordinary work, 'The undivided universe: an ontological interpretation of quantum theory'.

– Here we are.

Leaning with one arm resting on the shelf, the other holding the book about as far away as was possible, Pfrumpy began reading aloud.

– 'We have seen that some kind of nonlocality is common to all interpretations of the quantum theory . . . . nevertheless there have been persistent and strong objections to the consideration of nonlocal theories of any kind, usually with the hope that a local interpretation will sooner or later be possible. The general mode of explanation that is currently propagated in science is either action through contact or else action propagated continuously by fields. Anything more than this is often regarded as incompatible with the very possibility of doing science . . . . we have not yet found what we could regard as a valid logical or scientific reason for dismissing nonlocality. We are therefore led to ask' – Bohm does get rather too regal with that 'we', don't you think? – 'whether there could be some other kind of reason. It may well be that one of the main reasons that people dislike the concept of nonlocality can be found in the history of science. There was a long struggle to get free from what may perhaps have been regarded as *primitive superstitions* and *magical notions*[82] in which nonlocality played a key part. Perhaps there has remained a deep fear that the mere consideration of nonlocality might reopen the flood gates for what are felt to be irrational thoughts that lurk barely beneath the surface of modern culture.'

Pfrumpy looked up.

– I like that. That deep fear. Fear can be wholesome in times of ease. Actually it turns out that the scientists are our new medicine men, they are the shamans, not the artists or priests, who do most to sustain the idea of the miraculous. Which is why they should embrace nonlocality, to secure their position as mediators between human and divine. Well, Bohm does . . . there's a lot more here, and it's so readable because Bohm is all visionary priest, a shaman, reading him is like eavesdropping on the background of God's mind.

Pfrumpy leafed through the book.

– Listen to this, another of what Bohm calls his 'plausible conjectures'. This may not be Bohm at his most plausible, but it's certainly Bohm at his most original:

'One could suppose that in addition to the known types of field there was a new kind of field which would determine a space-like surface along which nonlocal effects would be propagated instantaneously. A good candidate for such a frame could be obtained by considering at each point in space-time the line connecting it to the presumed origin of the universe. This would determine a unique time order for the neighbourhood of that point around which one would expect isotropic properties in space. We may plausibly conjecture that this frame would be the one in which the 3K background radiation [83] in space has an isotropic distribution... in this frame there will evidently be no limit to the possible speed of the particles . . . our ontological approach allows us to consider the possibility that the current quantum mechanics is an approximation to a deeper theory . . . the long range connections of distant systems are not truly nonlocal, as implied by quantum theory, but are actually carried in the preferred frame at a speed that is finite but very much greater than that of light . . . ' and so on. Now could there have been some such frame in operation that might explain the nature of the connection between Alexanderplatz and Tempelhof?

– No.

– There was a tram connection once . . .

– It used to shuttle back and forth, but then it ran into a wall that someone stupidly built there.

Everyone laughed.

Pfrumpy raised a hand.

– The general mode of explanation that is currently propagated in science, says Bohm, is either action through contact or else action propagated continuously by fields. Well, what about this 'action continuously propagated by fields'? Planck's discovery of the quantum had already raised a question mark about continuity. Bohm, like Zeno, Nagarjuna and other great thinkers, believes it's an illusion. He says, here: 'One moment is all that there actually ever is. When any moment is, its past is always gone, and what remains of this past is only a trace. Its future is always 'not yet', but is still only a projection of an expectation. Then comes another moment, within which the earlier moment is likewise contained as a trace, while the later moment contains not only a part of what was previously projected, but also something new and not thus projected. In addition, it has in it, of course, a projection of still later moments. In other words, every moment has its past and its future, and the general features of the relationship of each moment to this past and this future are universally shared by all moments. Thus the space-time order of events is basically contained within each moment, in the sense that this order is implied by the inner structure of any event in the total process. Not only the time order but also the space order are implicit in this way. Now let us ask, 'Does a photon pass through the space between emitter and absorber?' The answer is that it does not. Of course, in large-scale experiences with objects moving at low velocities, typical processes will have a very high order trembling movement that is, for practical purposes, continuous. Extrapolation of this experience then leads us to expect that any influence whatsoever that passes from one point to another must go through a non-countable infinity of points. But is there any evidence that this infinity of points exists outside our customary map of space and time? In our theory, only the actual physical points need be considered (i.e. those at which an action of some kind takes place), so that there is no reason why a photon cannot connect two such points *without passing through any intermediate points*'.

CHAPTER
16.11

— Wow.

Pfrumpy closed the book and returned it to its place on the shelf. There was a longish pause as the room digested what Bohm had left in it.

— The trouble with Bohm is -

— I can see how -

Jens and Sommerfeld both began speaking at once. Jens backed down and let Sommerfeld continue.

— The problem with Bohm is that he wants to have it both ways. He *says* nonlocality, but I mean, once you propose time and space orders implicit in an *inner structure of events*, you are really letting locality in by the back door, aren't you.

— But that's just the point. Bohm says it's precisely the most characteristic quantum properties such as nonlocality and undivided wholeness that bring about the classical world with its locality and separability into distinct components. The one grows out of the other.

— How does it manage to do that?

— The classical 'world' emerges from quantum theory more or less — unscathed, I guess one might say. Its autonomy becomes apparent whenever the quantum potential can be neglected, i.e. pretty much for the entirety of our everyday lives, so that the classical world can be treated on its own, as if it were independently existent...

— Isn't it? The moon isn't there when no one's looking?

— No. I don't know. The eye can be sensitive to a few quanta at a time, but the reception of a small number of quanta gives only the vaguest sense of optical stimulation, not enough to create the forms of the classical world we're familiar with. Meaningful perception requires a very large number of quanta and therefore an essentially classic behaviour. The world of fields and particles, says Bohm, is what conveys information to our senses in a well-defined way. It's a question of degree. Through a process of amplification and recording in the stable structure of a measuring apparatus, such as the eye, the overall quantum 'world' can manifest itself in the more limited classical 'sub-world.' Because the classical world of locality is the one we inhabit with all our perceptions, this is the world we see as the real world, and the nonlocal quantum world as a limiting case of this. Bohm sees it the other way round. For him the quantum world constitutes *a more basic reality* than does the classical.

— More basic?

Pfrumpy intervened.

— Underlying all this is unbroken wholeness, even though our civilisation has developed in such a way as to strongly emphasise the separation into parts. That was Bohm's view, and in the end it's all the view you need to see.

— Was Bohm a Buddhist?

— Of course he was.

Pfrumpy smiled.

— Although he may not have seen it quite like that himself.

Wilma stretched and got up.

— I'm going to bed.

On her way through the door she stopped and turned round.

— You still haven't answered Frank's question, by the way.

— Frank's question?

— How did your photons manage it? What was the trick? You still haven't told us the answer. But I think the trick is just a kind of natural kinship, you know, quite natural, just falling into place along the lines of love. The world stands still. Good night everyone.

Wilma went out of the room, leaving an astonished silence behind her.

One by one they all peeled off and went, either home or to bed, until it was just the two of us, me and Frank down there. We got rather drunk, then hungry, ate what was left of the cold curry and drank some more again. At some point we must have gone upstairs. I had no recollection of our transit to the second floor, but a clear image of Frank flopping down and lying sprawled out on a yellow chaise longue. Then he went out, asleep just like that.

In a state near sleep myself, yet a part of me wide awake, everything emptied from my mind but the sight of Frank's cheek turned up to the lamp over the chaise longue. It caught all the light, showing the smoothness of the skin and a coil of soft down on it, little coils or spirals, in-curling waves of fine blonde hair more like a woman's than a man's. This was the cheek of a girl, girl or boy, it made no difference as Frank had apparently never needed to shave in his life. The other side of Frank lay hidden in the dark, all I saw was the side turned to me in the light. In the warmth of the light cone a residue of scent had been released, some sort of eau de cologne that Frank wore and which I recognised. I looked at Frank to the accompaniment of a feeling, a sort of colouring, with which I had never looked at him before. The colouring was desire.

Prompted, apparently, by the sight of soft down and the scent that came up off his cheek, although in a deeper sense by the ambivalence of Frank's sexual nature, it came unbidden but quite ready, completely formed, without hesitation or ambiguity itself, as if it had been awaiting this summons, detained only by my ignorance of it hitherto. I leaned forward and brushed the cheek with my lips; and all of me, body and mind, went out to Frank in a sort of exhalation of relief. I remained kneeling on the floor, my face hovering over his face, breathing it in, until I sat back on my heels for another look at him.

He opened his eyes. I was caught in the act.

How long had he been awake? Had my lips on his cheek awoken him? I now had the distinct impression he had been awake all the time, pretending to be asleep only to give my desire, and perhaps his own, its opportunity, his question the full reach of its significance.

– Who *are* you?

Frank now became the observer, I the observed.[84]

CHAPTER
17

Call me K.

An observer cannot observe without at the same time becoming a participant. An observer cannot avoid becoming involved. Yet from the age of five, when my parents escaped to the West via a tunnel from East Berlin and I went to live with my aunt, I had persuaded myself that I could. On the other side of the wood, beyond the fields behind the village where I lived with my aunt, ran the border, a scar you could tell from far away by the absence of life, earth scorched by a gigantic blow lamp, an emptiness across the landscape in its wake.

I never had any need of such fences or walls. I was never a security risk. In the hermetic world I constructed around me, I built the walls myself.

At the age of five, however, I may have constituted a security risk. In the group of escapees, whose plan required them to wait in the tunnel in total silence for anything up to thirty-six hours, there was no place for a small child. Later the child would understand this, as he would also understand the need for keeping the plan secret, including from himself.

For the year prior to the escape a routine had been carefully established. On Saturday my mother drove me out to my aunt's, where we stayed the night. But on the evening in question, after she had put me to bed, she walked to the station and caught the train back, leaving the car outside the house as her alibi, me to my bewilderment, and I never saw her or my father again.

Twenty years later, when she knew she was dying and no longer had anything to fear, my aunt told me the details of my mother's departure, which she had withheld from me at the time; how my mother cried so much she was barely able to summon the strength to leave the house, promising they would fetch me as soon as they had got over, pay a ransom or plan my escape, move heaven and earth – 'by hook or by crook and however long it took', the rhyme became a mantra I would repeat to myself for many years – they would arrange for me to join them in the West.

Of course there was no question of my aunt telling me such things *at the time*, not even to console me. To do so would have meant a security risk. Her own livelihood was at stake. Besides, my practically minded aunt knew these promises were already broken before they were made, flights of a nervous mother's fancy that would never come to anything.

I practised lying as still as death under my bed, imagining it was a tunnel, it seemed to me for hours, but I couldn't be quite sure because at some point I inevitably fell asleep. When I was twelve and took part in a survival exercise of a junior army division, the young pioneers, I lay hidden in a thicket without moving for twenty-four hours, but what did that prove, for by then I was twelve and no longer five.

In the end the results of all the tunnel tests I did no longer mattered. What mattered was that my mother had chosen, and that she had not chosen me.

After my military service I went to Berlin to study physics at Humboldt University. Thinking from this particular child's point of view about such things as Pauli's Exclusion Principle, the wave-particle duality, the paths chosen by a photon in the double-slit experiment, I finally accepted the parameters of the world inside my head, what it was that I needed to clarify, and decided I was temperamentally better suited to moral philosophy than physical science. Such child-to-man, person-to-profession transmutations are the business of human life, what the physicist Stapp in the context of collapsing the wave function called 'the evolution of its potentialities'.[85]

Two years after my aunt died the Wall came down, though not for me. I did not feel liberated, because, in the aftermath of my early abandonment by my parents, freedom was not something I could go to but which could only ever come to me, freely, that is, of its own accord.

I had no desire to go to the West. I was still waiting for the West, redeeming me as it had pledged, to keep its promise and come to me.

These are the qualities that make for a good observer – patience, stillness, withdrawal, the suppression of one's own will to the extremity of a passiveness mimicking death, as weaker creatures will do to deceive their predators – anything so as not to disturb what one observes and is trying to nurture into becoming, 'the evolution of its potentialities', freely and of its own accord.

Frank did not have such qualities – quite the opposite. He was not made out to be an observer, as I was, and it wasn't long before we reverted to our established roles.

CHAPTER
17.1

This late-night 'confession', however, if that isn't too melodramatic a word, which I made to Frank about myself (for that matter about Frank, too, or about my feelings for him), transformed the relationship between us. The discovery that we both lacked something, were both 'incomplete people', to use Frank's phrase, revealed what we had in common, and something in common is the basis of empathy – a sense of what one has in common being the *lack* of something far more so than a sense of its *possession*.

Dispossession among the poor has always led to a greater social solidarity than has possession among the rich, as I began to appreciate only after the fall of the Wall reunited us with our affluent relatives in the West.

Dispossessed, in effect, of my childhood, I had recourse to my imagination. For years I continued to adopt the attitude of deathlike passivity of an animal seeking to remain unnoticed by its predators – in winter lying motionless for hours under my bed, in summer in the woods, imagining myself to be in a tunnel where under pain of death I must lie completely still to escape detection.

Although I had motives that may have made mine an unusual case, I do not think that the behaviour of the sixteen or seventeen million compatriots who had remained with me in the country after everyone else had left was all that different from mine. Almost all of us, in our different ways, practised a sort of mimicry of death to avoid detection in life.

My childish imagination could put me into the situation of an animal feigning death, lying in a tunnel as still as possible in order to escape detection – and to all intents and purposes I became that animal, I lay in that tunnel, and in a way it was just another make-believe game, one that I habitually played. But this make-believe was in such earnest, without any exaggeration a matter of life and death, that the habit became ingrained and I never grew out of it, or the habit out of me.

Looking and listening around me, as I grew up into the role of observer for which I was destined by my aloof and non-committal nature, I realised that make-believe continued to occupy hardly less important a part in adults' lives than it did in the lives of children.

The language of the daily round of events was littered with its remnants – *like, as if, similar to*, everyday phrases worn deep both by and into people's thinking habits, mind-steps trodden by everyone without exception – and was subject to frequent intrusion by metaphors and tropes (many of them, in the relentlessly materialistic and plebeian society I was brought up in, dealing with sports, sex or technology) even in the talk of the least imaginative of individuals. Metaphors and tropes weren't luxuries, adornments. They were the stuff itself.

Outside of mathematics, there was no alternative to figures of speech. Outside of mathematics, the language of physics was as figurative as it was everywhere else, and in the end perhaps mathematics was a trope itself.

To people living inside a walled state the habit of comparison with people living outside it comes easily, one might say: inescapably. One might say they have a particular aptitude for it, schooled by their leaders' constant harping on the differences between conditions inside the wall and conditions outside it (they were always worse). But that really didn't interest me one way or the other. That didn't seem to me to be the point.

The point was that life within the walled state was always either like or unlike what was outside it.

Beyond likeness or unlikeness, life was apparently unable to exist. There was no life just by itself.

CHAPTER
17.12

Within this walled state (be it only the scarf-skin to wrap around a body), whose inmates had to rely more than usually on their imagination, it seemed to me that the tropes and metaphors seeking to establish connections were like hooked lines cast out over the walls into a surrounding dark, where sometimes they stuck fast.

An unlikeness no less than a likeness could serve to establish what was in common; something in common was the basis of empathy, the basis of empathy was the duality of everything that existed. In the dual view of existence, everything that is could only have its existence in terms of what it was not. I am like, or unlike, therefore I am.

It was with some such view in mind that I had already begun to think of *entanglement* when I arrived in Berlin to take up my studies. Left to my own devices, my own worn thinking habits, I wouldn't have got very far with my project. Without the friendship of Frank, the mindset I observed and adopted from Pfrumpy, from Wilma hardly any less, I wouldn't have arrived anywhere at all. The metaphor for their own life, their death no less, was a bridge, and it was by means of this bridge that I crossed over into their company.

CHAPTER
18

During the months-long shooting of the Pissoir and Palace-of-the-Republic series, Wilma had early recognised a fault line in Frank's nature, which she had seen verified in the two years since: the lack of a personal volition in Frank, of wanting anything particular from life. He roamed around in his vagrant existence, a stray dog lifting his leg in basements and underground shafts, dirty and derelict places, busy now with one thing, now with another, none of them indispensable to him, they could equally well have been something else. There was a lack of the act of consummation, taking up into his life all those things he had unearthed at the bottom of it, finding a place for them as part of a coherent personal history, furnishings that documented the reality of Frank's tenure, in possession of his own life.

In Frank's fascination with opening up things that were closed, revitalising condemned houses and disused air raid shelters or digging up things buried in the ground, Wilma had sensed, beyond the curiosity, also the fear of what he would find. The fault line she saw in Frank's nature, shot through as it was with an awareness of the expendability of all that he did, was more than just a lack of expectation of anything definite from life. What nourished Frank's vitality was the prospect of its extinction.

Wilma was a little afraid of telling Frank what was about to happen to her. She wanted Pfrumpy to be there when she told him, and perhaps because she anticipated Frank making some kind of a scene, or perhaps because she was worried she would have difficulty telling him when they were alone, she preferred their conversation to take place in public.

On a warm October afternoon the three of them sat outside at one of the sidewalk cafe tables on the Q-Damm. Wilma had been intending to lead up to it, circuitously, as if in Wilma's scheme of things there was a world in which it might have been possible to break the news of her death gently to Frank, but it came out against her will in a couple of shorn and flat sentences, a blunt weapon that struck Frank straight through the heart.

For Frank, at least as he would later describe it to K., the sun immediately clouded over, in its penumbra the day turned cold. Buildings not so very tall seemed suddenly to huddle together and lengthen, casting long shadows like skyscrapers, and between them a rapidly deepening obscurity dropped down in narrow wells ending in pools of dark. In what ground level patchwork was left of the light he sat immobilised, frozen to his chair on the pavement of the Q-Damm. His heart seemed to have stopped. Momentarily he experienced the cessation of all things – the sound of traffic, footsteps, coffee cups, the movement of people around him and branches in the tree overhead, all momentarily suspended – and the rush of their recommencement in his consciousness some time later overwhelmed him with their sudden and violent eruptive noise. Frank felt he had to get up and actually *shout down the noise* in order to make himself heard, as he explained later, with apologies to Wilma and Pfrumpy for giving them such a shock.

In an ordinary tone of voice Frank said:

– When you go we go too, of course, but you know that, Eurydice.

And then, shouting:

– *We all go down together!*

Alarmed by Frank's outburst, a child at the next table began crying, a waiter came hurrying out of the cafe and the people at the sidewalk tables, turning their heads quickly to see what had happened, thought the child must be crying because the man standing there had been shouting at it.

K. wondered whether Frank really did have any such experience at the time, or whether, inspired by the sort of self-dramatisation to which Frank was prone, it only later took shape in Frank's consciousness in the telling, only bodied out, as it were, with words he had spoken mainly to create an effect. Going down – what sort of an expression was that?

When he told him on the phone about the conversation with Wilma in the cafe that morning, Frank at any rate passed on to K. what Wilma had said to him and what he had said to Wilma verbatim, the words *we all go down together*. K. initially had his doubts about this, too, perhaps in his own way being as inclined to caution as Frank was to showmanship. But how else would Frank most naturally approach the subject of Wilma's death if not through a figure of speech that had so long been established in his relationship with Wilma, the story of Eurydice going down into the underworld? What story dramatised better the unbearable loneliness of the survivor of a lost love?

K. noted that Frank's version offered yet another variant of the original story. Eurydice had died of snakebite, and the passage of Orpheus to Hades, after pleading and obtaining exemption for her from the gods, was to retrieve her and restore her to the upper world. But Frank was not thinking of rescuing Wilma from the underworld or doing anything quaintly mythological like that, just of Pfrumpy and himself sharing with Wilma her extinction as the only way out, to unburden themselves of an unendurable loneliness.

Ever since he had been deserted by his mother, K. had his doubts about a number of things.

K. didn't believe in any sort of going down together, to Hades or by any subterranean means across any other sort of border to whatever other destination. Werther or Kleist might have done so in another age, and nowadays there were perhaps adolescents who still did. That kind of thing was just Romantic posturing. K. found the memory of the perpetrators of all such border crossings detestable.

Frank spoke to K. on this subject at length, however, always on the cool assumption that *cause precedes effect*, that Wilma's death somehow *led on inescapably* to his own, making all the more striking Frank's subsequent admission that the disclosure of Wilma's impending death had given him a feeling of 'enormous relief'.

K. wouldn't take Frank at his word in any of these statements, believing the substitution of words that never failed Frank for emotional responses that always did to be part and parcel of his showman personality, which K. managed to disapprove of even as he admired and envied it. He had always admired a sort of negligence Frank cultivated, from the way he wore a scarf to the equal footing he assumed for himself in the company of his professors. It was in character for Frank to display the same lassitude in leaving life as he had in living it, but K. regarded such an attitude as just another pose.

In truth, K. was jealous of Wilma and the hold she had over Frank. For this reason he chose to downplay Frank and Wilma and the whole affair. This will never happen, he told himself.

K. wished that he too could have experienced an 'enormous relief' himself and be rid of the past and live at peace with himself.

Perceiving what K. apparently didn't see, Frank's bottom-line fear of the yawning abyss, and discerning in such drawing back from the brink just the opposite attraction, namely a desire to step over it, Wilma was equally sure he meant what he said.

There was a part of Wilma that could sympathise with the 'enormous relief' Frank had admitted to after she told him she was going to die, for she had felt something like it herself. In Frank's position, it was much easier to disengage voluntarily from life if one had never felt particularly attached to it. Particularly attached as Frank had only ever really been to Wilma, but being otherwise, according to his own estimate, expendable in his existence, it was not the relinquishing of life that would entail any sacrifice for Frank, it would be having to hang on to a life in which there was no Wilma.

There was a great deal in her life to which Wilma felt very deeply attached, however, beginning with Pfrumpy and Frank and extending to much more. But as she walked down the road, still in something of a daze after leaving the clinic, the clairvoyant Wilma had experienced her own flash of relief that the blight man was born for had come to her at last, in the definite shape of a cancer of which she was bound to die. *That's me settled*, she might even have thought to herself at the time, *I'm done*. Given assurance by this certainty, or just obliterated by it, Wilma's anxieties regarding the unknown blight or blights she might yet have to face were exorcised in a flash of relief, knowing she faced those anxieties no longer.

It wasn't that Wilma wanted Frank or Pfrumpy to die, no more herself, but neither did she want them to survive her when she was no longer. Whether this was just a metaphor for human inseparability in jeopardy through death, for a deep-rooted human desire that loyalty should be undying, or whether Wilma truly understood and accepted the consequence of the stark naked deed that had to follow from such a resolution – and it did cross her mind, vividly, the butterflies in her stomach before the leap, the spattered piecemeal skull on the pavement after it, the gun barrel exploding in the smithereens of a mouth, or, worst of all, the methodical and total humiliation by autopsy if you tried to sneak out under cover of an overdose – Wilma was unable to say because she chose not to dwell on such things.

There are no clear wishes. Such clarity does not happen. Every wish is in two minds, like the particles in the double-slit experiment.

Without need for discussion, Frank and Wilma were in agreement about what it was they wanted. They did not want to wait. They wanted it to end and they would choose their own moment, or, even better, have it chosen for them, and they anticipated that moment not entirely without a thrill of fear, but also not entirely without a thrill of furtive joy.

CHAPTER
18.1

Frank had been making certain assumptions in his use of 'we', and Wilma seemed tacitly to be assenting. But Pfrumpy himself had so far said nothing. From Pfrumpy there had been no mention of any 'going down' with Wilma. When Frank had suddenly spoken in tongues at the cafe on the Q-Damm Pfrumpy had not seconded Frank, nor had he opposed him. He had abstained.

Wilma assured Frank, uneasy in the face of this silence, that Pfrumpy would be 'all right'.

Meanwhile Pfrumpy carried on with his daily routine as if nothing had changed. In collaboration with Babaji, he had recently completed a new annotated translation of the *Tibetan Book of the Dead*, which in Babaji's absence — he was on holiday in Switzerland with his granddaughter — Pfrumpy was now preparing for publication. While Frank and Wilma sat and walked and talked their way through the deepening conspiracy of the fall, imagining their forthcoming departure from the world and how they would arrange it, the third party to their plan was closeted in the library, peering at microfilms, all day and sometimes all night too. Wilma was familiar with these periodic reversions to hermitic life, cave retreats, she called them, and waited for Pfrumpy to come out.

But Frank's increasingly histrionic style was getting on Pfrumpy's nerves, something it wasn't easy to do. Frank had discovered a new role he liked, a doomsday flippancy, he aired macabre observations around the house and had it been possible — there was of course a taboo on discussing *going down* outside their own circle, applying particularly to

Frank and particularly in the presence of K. – he would have hawked them around town too. But being the indiscreet person he was, and having in the meantime become almost as intimate with K. as he was with Wilma and Pfrumpy, Frank had naturally told K. what was going on.

Frank had a list of desirable options as to when, where, how, in black and white or colour, he even looked though magazines in search of a venue that took his fancy. He had made a career for himself as an exhibitionist, even when he was doing science.

In that light here was nothing reproachable about Frank's obsession with finding for his death the right *mise-en-scène* he had sought for his life, beginning with the new image of himself he had brought with him from the provinces when he first arrived in Berlin. This was, in essence, the same Frank making much the same contribution he had always made, bringing levity into what Babaji, at least, had felt to be an overseriousness in Wilma's life with Pfrumpy, but Pfrumpy was no longer grateful or amused. Sitting at the dinner table one night he found Frank's chatter sufficiently irritating to come bristling out of his cave, armed to the teeth.

Frank was holding forth in the usual vein.

– How about Venice? Any takers for death in Venice? A bit passé, a bit overdone? Last call for Venice, going, going...

Frank looked round the table before thumping it with his shoe.

– Gone.

Pfrumpy got up, went to the kitchen dresser and took a large, heavy revolver out of the bottom drawer.

– Here. Try it with this. At six inches it'll blow your head off, maybe shut you up too.

He laid the revolver on the table in front of Frank and went upstairs.

For several days the revolver remained lying on the table where Pfrumpy had left it while he continued to taunt Frank.

– Go on. It's loaded. All you have to do is pull the trigger, Frank. It's *very easy to do*.

But it was just this *very easy to do* that Frank found scary. It should be hard to do, or what was it worth? When the gun disappeared from the kitchen table, Frank was secretly relieved.

Over the next few days, however, it began turning up in other odd places around the house where Pfrumpy had left it, in the wash basin of the downstairs toilet, on the landing carpet and the yellow chaise longue in Frank's room. Pfrumpy pointed it out to him in case he had missed it and winked conspiratorially at Frank.

One night he discovered it lying under his pillow.

Should the desire come upon him at night, said Pfrumpy, actually waking Frank up to tell him this, then he gave Frank permission to shoot him in his sleep. It was his understanding Wilma would give her permission too. Then all Frank needed was permission from himself.

Frank began to find the revolver business unnerving, Wilma too.

Whenever Pfrumpy held a hand to his head, crooked his finger and said 'Bang!' Wilma jumped.

— For God's sake Pfrumpy, stop it! Can't you just get rid of the damn thing?

That was the last they saw of Pfrumpy's revolver.

But Frank had been shaken by Pfrumpy's cold-bloodedness and was cured of his posturing before he jeopardised their undertaking by turning it into a farce.

CHAPTER
19

The morning after my late-night conversation with Frank — it may already have been afternoon — I went upstairs with him to see if Wilma and Pfrumpy wanted to have breakfast with us. Wilma was closeted in her darkroom, Babaji busy with manuscripts in the library. We went on up to the tower room. A thin quilt lay on the floor where Pfrumpy slept.

Pfrumpy was sitting out on the roof terrace without any clothes on, as was always his habit when meditating. A light smatter of snow had fallen in the night and dusted the surrounding roofs. It was freezing outside.

I wondered how Pfrumpy withstood the cold. It was on this occasion that I learned from him about the practice of *gTum-mo*, the production of so called psychic heat by a combination of breathing exercises while concentrating on the element fire.

Pfrumpy had discovered *gTum-mo* during the years in Ladakh. He told me that it was an indispensable technique for monks living in the extreme cold of the mountains. Advanced practitioners could drape soaking cloths around them in freezing weather and dry the cloths with their own body heat. They even held competitions. Like other apparently miraculous powers exploited by fakirs in the market places, *gTum-mo* had been degraded as a stunt, bringing it into disrepute. Notwithstanding, among serious practitioners it served incidentally as an aid to yoga meditation.[86]

What was yoga? I knew nothing about these things.

According to Pfrumpy, the Sanskrit word *yoga* meant union, a yoking together, whereas the Tibetan word *naljor* meant abiding naturally, just being oneself.

This introduction to yoga appealed to me because it coincided with my own ideas of things being as they were only by virtue of the possibility of their being something else.[87]

Yoga as practised by Pfrumpy was enumerated as the Eightfold Path by Patanjali in his *Sutras*, to which I would be gradually introduced by Pfrumpy during the last eighteen months of his life.

The Eightfold Path circumscribed the following:

1) *yama* or moral conduct, non-injury to others, truthfulness, continence 2) *niyama* religious observance 3) *asana* or right posture (the spinal column straight) 4) *pranayama* (control of *prana*, the subtle life currents) 5) *pratyahara* (withdrawal of the senses from external objects).

The last three items in the Eightfold Path described forms of yoga proper, that is, its purely meditational rather than moral aspects: 6) *dharana*, concentration, holding the mind to one thought 7) *dhyana* or meditation and 8) *samadhi* (superconscious experience, leading to *kaivalya*, or absoluteness).

These unfamiliar terms were devoid of any real content for me when I first encountered them. They were untranslatable into any language I knew. They were metaphors, deeds masquerading as words. They were words for doing, not understanding. They referred to nothing in my experience. They were as good as meaningless.

This was why the geraniums that bloomed on Pfrumpy's terrace throughout the winter, doing rather than understanding, surviving without need of meaning, just being, acquired a particular significance on my own path to *samadhi*.

The qualities that make for a good observer – patience, stillness, withdrawal, the suppression of one's own will to the extremity of a passiveness mimicking death, as weaker creatures will do to deceive their predators, anything so as not to disturb what one observes and is trying to nurture into becoming – such qualities lend themselves equally to the self-discipline required by meditation.

Naturally Pfrumpy included the geraniums in his thoughts. Sheltered, as the flowers apparently were, within the heat cone of *gTum-mo* his body generated, they were warmed — one might say 'incidentally'. With his thoughts he also nourished the plants that lived alongside him in his roof-top eyrie, smoothed out leaves tending to crinkle in the cold, kept supple their roots.

Such transference of energy is known in yogic terminology as *trongjug*, one of the *siddhis*, or extraordinary feats of mind, which in the West go under the general name of psychokinesis.

A bugbear of conventional science, psychokinesis has long been admitted by science but cannot be explained in terms it finds satisfactory.[88] Unsatisfactory, the phenomenon is still there. Unexplained, unable to be accommodated by the logical constraints of science, it does not go away.

However, the phenomenon presents us with a problem only when an absolute division is made between the organism geranium and the organism Pfrumpy. But Pfrumpy did not live in a walled state, he lived in metaphors, with lines of communication, one might say bridges, docking onto everything around him.

When Pfrumpy raised with me the subject of *dharana*, the sixth way station on the Eightfold Path, it led us on to a discussion of concentration in general. In the West, he said, we understood by this a restriction of the movement of the mind to certain subjects, not the movement itself. In Eastern meditation *all* movement of the mind ceased, allowing it to fuse and become one with the object of its concentration.[89]

I asked Pfrumpy what those objects were, and he showed me as an example the smooth round stone he had brought back with him from a river-bed in Ladakh. This was the stone on which he had learned *dharana*. He kept it as a memento, although he no longer needed it in front of him in order to focus his mind, and before he died he gave it to me.

The movement of the mind did not cease all at once. From *dharana*, 'concentration', the sixth way station of the Eightfold Path, clearing the mind of turmoil and focusing it, the yogin moved on to the seventh, *dhyana*, or meditation, and from there to the eighth and last, the trance-like state known as *samadhi*. *Dhyana* was still movement, was indeed defined as flow: *tatra pratyaya-aikatanata dhyanam*. 'Uninterrupted flow (of the mind) towards the object (chosen for contemplation) is meditation.'[90]

The three taken together – *dharana*, *dhyana* and *samadhi* – constituted what was known as *samyama*.

Over a considerable period of time, after long and repeated efforts, I did myself eventually succeed in accomplishing *samyama* to a degree, whereas Pfrumpy, even while engaged with some other activity, was able to pass into the centre of his consciousness in *samyama* almost instantaneously.

The complete suspension of movement came only at the end of the Eightfold Path.

'The same (meditation) when there is consciousness only of the object of meditation and not of itself (the mind) is *samadhi*.'[91]

'The first aspect of *samadhi* with which Patanjali deals is the distinction between *samprajnata* (samadhi with *prajna* = *pra*, 'high', + *jna*, 'knowing', meaning higher consciousness working through the mind in all its stages) and *asamprajnata samadhi*. The characteristic of this higher consciousness which unfolds in samadhi is that the mind is cut off completely from the physical world, free from the interference of the physical brain. In *samprajnata samadhi* there is a *pratyaya* ('seed')[92] in the field of consciousness and the consciousness is fully directed to it. So the direction of consciousness is from the centre outwards. In *asamprajnata samadhi* there is no 'seed' and therefore nothing to draw the consciousness outwards [93] and hold it there. So as soon as the *pratyaya* (P) is dropped or suppressed, the consciousness begins to recede to its centre and after passing momentarily through this centre tends to emerge into the next, subtler vehicle. When this process has been completed the *pratyaya* (P[1]) of the next higher plane appears, and the direction of the consciousness again becomes from the centre outwards, and so on. The void of *asamprajnata samadhi* between these 'seeded' states is sometimes called a 'cloud'. The recession of consciousness towards its centre is thus not a steady and uninterrupted sinking into greater and greater depths, but consists in this alternate outward and inward movement of consciousness at each barrier separating the two planes.

'It should be noted that throughout the recession of consciousness in the four stages there is always something in the field of consciousness. It is true that during the phase of *asamprajnata samadhi* there is no seed but only a cloud or void, but these too constitute a cover on pure consciousness. It is only this blurred impression produced in consciousness when it passes through the critical phase between the seeds of two successive planes. This phase is rather like the critical state between two states of matter, liquid and gaseous, when it can be called neither liquid nor gaseous . . .'[94]

'To be able to jump from one plane to another, the mind must first be brought to that condition in which it is without movement through 'shining' with the object which holds the field of consciousness.'[95]

' *'Nirodha parinama* is that transformation of the mind in which it becomes progressively permeated by that condition of *nirodha* which intervenes momentarily between an impression which is disappearing and the impression which is taking place.'[96]

'Nirodha is that momentary unmodified state of the mind which intervenes when one impression which holds the field of consciousness is replaced by another impression. Between two successive impressions there must be a momentary state in which the mind has no impression at all. The object of *nirodha parinama* is to produce at will this momentary state and gradually extend it, so that the mind can exist for a considerable duration in this unmodified state. In passing from a condition in which the 'seed' of samadhi holds the field of consciousness to a condition of complete *nirodha*, there is a struggle between two opposite tendencies, the tendency of the 'seed' to rise again in the field of consciousness and the tendency of the mind to remain in the condition of *nirodha*. As the definition of *samadhi parinama* shows, its essential nature is the gradual reduction of the all-pointed condition of the mind to the one-pointed condition.'[97]

CHAPTER
19.1111

'Then, again, the condition of the mind in which the 'object' (in the mind) which subsides is always exactly similar to the 'object' which arises in the next moment is called *ekagrata parinama*.' [98]

'The characteristic of this *ekagrata parinama* is that exactly the same *pratyaya* (seed) rises in the field of consciousness again and again and produces the impression as if a single fixed unchanging *pratyaya* is occupying the field. The succession of exactly similar images in an apparently stationary *pratyaya* is due to the intermittent nature of the manifested universe. It appears and disappears alternately, but the interval, called a *ksana*, is so small that it appears to be a continuous phenomenon. It is not only in *samadhi* that this discontinuity enters in the perception of the *pratyaya*. It is present in all perceptions. Wherever there is manifestation there must be discontinuity or succession or underlying process, which is called *kramah* (law of nature). It is because the phenomenon is dynamic and not static that it is called a *parinama* (transformation) and not *avastha* (state).' [99]

CHAPTER
19.1112

Naturally all workings of the mind, like all things language says, can be expressed only by metaphors.

The rendering of any thing by any word is itself a metaphor.

The very nature of language is metaphor.

Seeds in the field of consciousness, the alternation of seeded and unseeded states, subsiding and arising with intermittent states that were void, containing nothing unless perhaps a cloud, leaps from one plane of consciousness to another corresponding to the discontinuous nature of the manifest universe: naturally such metaphors called to mind the strikingly similar figures of speech – quantal transitions or quantum leaps from one eigenstate to another with nothing in-between, a void comparable to the momentary states in which the mind had no impression at all – that were employed by the founders of quantum mechanics some thousands of years after Patanjali had conceived his *Sutras*.[100]

If yoga described the activity of mind and quantum mechanics the activity of matter in figures of speech that had so much in common, equating the one with the other, then the inference was this could only be so because what the figures of speech had in common the activities they figured had in common with them.

With equal justification one could say that yoga described matter and quantum mechanics described mind, the one shining with the other.

That the mind must first be brought to that condition in which it is without movement through 'shining' with the object which holds the field of consciousness was, for me, the most illuminating of these figures of speech.

I could imagine, for example – bearing in mind the instantaneous sharing of knowledge by entangled pairs of particles, and assuming the key to such instantaneous sharing was not speed of movement but lack of the need for any movement at all – that a kind of shining might have its place in the solution to the puzzle of the twin-photon experiment.

It cast its own light on descriptions of shining experiences among seers at all times and in all places, from Jakob Boehme and Swedenborg to Einstein and Heisenberg. Where there was consciousness only of the object of meditation and not of the meditating mind, there was suspension of all movement and a shining with that object.

Disappearance of the mind's self-awareness was called by Patanjali *svarupa sunyam iva*. *Svarupa* meant the own-nature or essence of a thing, *sunyam* meant void, *iva* as if.

This I could understand.

'Own-nature as if void.'

In this final figure of speech the thinker-thought distinction was dissolved, in their shining the two became one, Swedenborg and his Cloud, Heisenberg and his Uncertainty Principle, Pfrumpy and his boxes of geraniums.

CHAPTER
19.2

Pfrumpy, as I have mentioned, kept a journal of sorts, in which he made jottings, for the most part incoherent. Typically there would be a single word accompanied by an exclamation mark, the signature tune of the writer in a moved state of mind.

chair! blue!

These words were dashed off, sometimes quite illegibly. On page 10 of the pale blue notebook, manufactured with handmade paper and bearing the stamp of an upmarket stationery supplier in Wilmersdorf, about two-thirds of which remained unfilled, we find the single word 'bridge', without an exclamation mark and in a perfectly sober handwriting. Perhaps for this reason it manages to look subdued alongside all its rollicking curlicue companions.

Pfrumpy formed the letters of this word in a spirit clearly different from the spirit in which he formed the letters of other words. He has omitted to give it his signature tune. Where all the other words have been impetuously dashed off, this one looks as if it had been written in cold blood.

Bridge.

Once I had gained regular access to the tower room, from about the spring of the year before Pfrumpy died, I could myself observe directly a process that until then I had been able to put together only second-hand from the observations of others. This later enabled me to make sense of entries in Pfrumpy's diary that would otherwise have been unintelligible.

One such observation was the *series of photos* piled on a table in the tower room for some days during that summer.

At first sight, they were unremarkable photos, just snapshots of one of our local landmarks. Only the first few of them showed it in its entirety, including the background which made it the landmark it was.

Then the camera moved in closer, showed girders, a balustrade, and then, apparently still closer in, just bits of these, a blur lacking any features that would have enabled one to guess what one was looking at unless one knew the series of images to which they belonged.

There must have been several dozen of these photos, a big stack of them, perhaps as many as fifty or so.

What they showed was Glienicker Bridge.

chair! blue!

Another observation that later helped me to interpret entries in Pfrumpy's diary was an inventory of the things that accompanied him in his daily life. The ceiling of the tower room was painted a glowing marine blue. And I had little doubt the chair referred to in the diary was the rather squat antique chair with short curving legs and a broad fretted back splat leaning out at an obtuse angle, rather like a pregnant woman with a hand behind her to support her back, which stood by the bedroom door.

It was indeed a chair for pregnant women, Pfrumpy afterwards told me, remarking on the curious similarity to a pregnant woman the chair itself possessed, which had also struck me. It had belonged to his grandmother. She had sat in it when pregnant and later when nursing his father. Shining with the chair, it was quite conceivable to me that Pfrumpy had shone also with the woman who had sat in it and whom he had never seen in his life.

stone!

Obviously this was the stone from the river bed in Ladakh. It sat on Pfrumpy's shelf of curiosities above his bed. In retrospect, these observations came together in my head to present themselves in an arrangement I instinctively felt was right.

At one time or another the objects named had all served Pfrumpy as 'seeds' of meditation.

In *samprajnata samadhi* there was a seed in the field of consciousness and the consciousness was fully directed to it. Pfrumpy must have been shining not only with his geraniums, chair, stone, blue, grandmother and all the rest.

It was my conjecture that eighteen months before he died with Wilma and Frank in the car that plunged into the river Pfrumpy had also begun shining with Glienicker Bridge.

CHAPTER
19.21

'The photographs of the bridge, these he must rapidly have internalised, seeing in his mind's eye an image of the bridge with greater clarity than in any picture. In the deep stages of *samadhi*,' I ventured, growing bolder, 'progressing through layers of the material composition of the bridge, Pfrumpy would have penetrated to its core and discovered in the whirl of atoms there the flaws known as interstitials, those vacant sites which constituted its crystal structure, until he arrived at a microscopic crack and recognised in it the potential for what was known to the metallurgists who carried out the analysis as the 'initiation site' of metal fatigue — a metal cancer, so to speak, a terminal disease of which the bridge was one day bound to die.'

CHAPTER
20

Peabody smiled when I presented this view of the case to him. It was the first time I had seen him smile at all during the two afternoons I had so far spent talking with him in his Montreal apartment. Far from bringing to his face anything like a sense of relaxation, the smile only emphasised how gaunt it had become.

– Well . . .

He sat pondering in a rocking-chair at a window that looked out over a line of trees, perhaps digesting the metal cancer I had unthinkingly introduced into the conversation.

Unbidden guests, police sirens, the shouts of children, a ball being kicked around, noises having nothing to do with the world the sick man inhabited, bounced up to us on the top floor of the rickety old house backing onto a park. In the thirty odd years he had lived there, Peabody said, he had watched the neighbourhood come down quite a bit but he had grown fond of the place and had no intention of moving, not at this stage of life.

– Being a practically minded man, without much imagination, I guess, I personally would go along with the finding of the inquiry they did at the time in Berlin, you know. Material damage, more serious than we at first realised, was done to the bridge when that truck backed into it. Seems to me a credible explanation for how the balustrade might have been sufficiently weakened for the car, you know, to have penetrated it, however slowly it would have been driving. So all this other stuff you bring up . . . I don't see much call for that.

We had been through all this often enough before, of course. I could have reminded Peabody that the truck had not even touched the balustrade. This was the whole point, the reason why he had himself arranged for a sample of the railing to be sent over from Berlin, years ago, and had commissioned a specialist report on the subject of metal fatigue. It was in fact that report which had been the starting point of my own inquiries. But Peabody's decline was so distressingly evident that I thought it better not to mention any of these things. It was Peabody's testimony I wanted to record on the tape, not my arguments with him.

— Anyway, what you're suggesting makes everything much worse for Pfrumpy, of course. You do realise that? You're saying that it wasn't an accident at all. You're saying — and if you are to be believed, what fantastic lengths he went to! — Pfrumpy drove the car off of that bridge deliberately, had long been, what shall we say, *planning* the deed? — the deliberate killing of three people, opening up an initiation site you would have us believe and paving a veritable highroad to their death. Murder. That's where your — shining, Jesus! — will land us. Well!

Peabody groped inside the pocket of his dressing-gown and pulled out a pack of cigarettes.

— Own-nature as if void. I can believe that, yes I can! Boy, does that ring a few bells! You said that own-nature as if void was what you learned from Pfrumpy, OK, so now we're on the subject, let's talk about *zombies* . . .

It was then that Peabody told me about Pfrumpy's early alcoholism, ending with a passage on the tape I would listen to so often that I had it by heart.

'Pfrumpy remained at bottom a reformed alcoholic, and as with all the reformed alcoholics I've known over the years it was the same in Pfrumpy's case, no exceptions, okay, so here's what I'm saying, the life spark seemed to have gone out of Pfrumpy, like a zombie, you know, a dead man resurrected but somehow not quite come back to life...'

I was profoundly shocked when I heard these revelations for the first time.

It wasn't made any better for me by Peabody's admitting to the envy he had felt for Pfrumpy's superior rich-boy status, his owning up to the flashes of 'deep hatred' with which their boyhood friendship had been flecked; and how, as a result, his view of Pfrumpy was freighted with all kinds of warping that in a court of law would have made him a witness whose credibility was easily demolished. Peabody's readiness to admit his own failings, to point out how prejudicial they were to his giving a fair view of Pfrumpy, had the opposite effect on me – no doubt calculated by the lawyer in Peabody – of making that view sound all the more persuasive.

– Nevertheless...where was I now? Look, for as long as we were kids there was never a time in my life when Pfrumpy wasn't around, all the way to college. We grew up together, we were like twins, hell, I practically watched him come out of his mother's womb. I *knew* this guy. School together, ball games, hockey, stealing candy from the corner store, the usual kind of thing. He was a generous kid. Whatever he had he shared with me. Very generous, and that hurt, because early on I recognised I wasn't. Cigarette?

– No thank you.

– It also reminded me I was the poor relation who got the hand-outs, and I kind of resented that, too. The other thing about Pfrumpy: unbelievably stubborn. We would fight, the way kids do, and I would have him pinned down, but he would never admit it. He never gave in, never backed down, never let go of something he had taken it into his mind to do. I don't know what it means when a person is, well, *unnaturally* stubborn, plain goddamn ornery we used to call it, but taken together with an almost profligate generosity it suggests to me an obsession with *power*.

Peabody poured himself a glass of water from the carafe on the table beside him, nursing the glass in his hands.

– There's a degree of stubbornness that makes a person kind of – unreachable. I mean, not quite human. They're stuck some place where no one else can get to them. Anyway, I only mention it in connection with this other thing about Pfrumpy as a kid.

– What was that?

– He was a bad loser.

— Bad loser?

— Bad loser. He just could — not — bear — to — *lose.*

Peabody rapped the armrest as he spoke each of these words with a pause between each of them for greater emphasis. He looked quite angry.

I changed the subject, asking him how Pfrumpy had managed to become an alcoholic at such an early age.

— Too much time on his hands. Too much money. A lack of perspective, of the need to get on with anything in particular. No lost love or anything dramatic like that. Without the discipline a working routine provides, you can just slide into it. There's a lot of booze all summer when rich people go to their cottages on the lakes. Usually the booze stays in the cupboard after they close down their summer houses and return to the city in the fall, that's sort of the done thing, but Pfrumpy got into the habit of bringing the booze back with him. And there was a history of alcoholism in the family, on his mother's side, which Pfrumpy may have inherited, who knows . . .

Peabody slumped back in his chair. So much talking had exhausted him.

CHAPTER
20.1

On my third visit to Peabody's apartment I asked him about his first encounter with Pfrumpy in the Himalayas after an absence of eight years, and their subsequent return to Montreal with Babaji. But Pea was having a bad day, he wandered, lost his way in his memory, said he just wanted to lie down and rest. I had to leave him after only an hour.

CHAPTER
20.2

The following day he was back on form, showing not a trace of the illness that had been closing in ominously the previous day. In the meantime, he must have given a lot of thought to the subject. He had made up his mind. His verdict on Pfrumpy was delivered like a prepared statement, as if he had it by heart.

— The man who returned to Montreal, went back to college and became the CEO of his father's company, was not the person who had left eight years earlier. Had he changed?

Exhaling, Peabody seemed to be watching his thoughts trail out with the smoke.

— I don't believe people change. It's not in human nature, not in nature at all. Do trees change? Not really. They realise their potential. What was in the acorn is the oak that comes out. Throughout his life Pfrumpy had always been a bit of a wild card, you know. He tended to the extreme, the unpredictable. When you can't live within the norm, you know, either way out leads you to an extreme. The alcoholic was followed by a teetotaller, the playboy by a hermit living in a cave who abstained from the world as obstinately as his predecessor had succumbed to every excess the world had to offer. This may sound like an old cynic talking, but now, between friends, what's really the difference?

He appealed to me with spread hands.

— I tried to find something about this new Pfrumpy that had remained familiar to me from the past, an ID sewn into the lining, kind of thing. But there was nothing there. Quite spooky. Pfrumpy seemed to have lost his personality. Where could it have gone? Nothing ruffled him. Nothing touched him. You couldn't reach him. He wasn't there. It was as if he had been brainwashed. If that's what you get for living alone in a cave for three years, count me out. Pal, you *said* it: own-nature as if void. A former alcoholic who had gone dry, his spirit sucked out of him, zombie is the only word for it. Except, *exce-e-pt*, for this one occasion . . .

Animated, Peabody paused to light another cigarette to keep him on pitch. The lighter didn't work. He asked me to fetch matches from the kitchen.

– Kids' party at the summer cottage of some mutual friends, all the neighbours had been invited, me and my ex-wife, Pfrumpy and Wilma were there too. We were playing cards with a bunch of these kids, eleven, twelve year-olds, the cards had pictures on them, OK, trees, animals, automobiles and stuff like that. You have to collect matching suits to win, and the winner goes to the lucky dip and pulls himself out a prize. Not a big deal. Well, there's one kid who hits lucky and keeps on winning, keeps on going back for more prizes, and with a consistency that was so remarkable we began to make jokes about it. Pfrumpy was always the runner-up, OK, always losing out to this lucky winner. Pfrumpy laughed along with the rest of us and made a big joke of it. But I was sitting right opposite Pfrumpy and I knew part of him wasn't laughing. Part of him was really mad. It only showed in his eyes. I remembered it from boyhood fights with Pfrumpy when I had him pinned on the ground and still he obstinately refused, *refused* to acknowledge he was beat. There it was again, something fixed and cold about the look in his eyes, and I thought, I've had to wait a *long time* for this but now I got you, Pfrumpy boy, same kid who always *was* a bad loser, you can be a playboy and turn yourself into a hermit, go off and live in a cave for years, whatever, and still never get shot of yourself, just can't be done, OK, because people don't change, people stay the same.

Peabody put his thumbnail on the smouldering butt and crushed the cigarette in the ashtray on his lap.

CHAPTER
20.3

By the last day the lawyer had talked himself to the heart of the matter and was ready to open the case for the prosecution.

— In all the uncertainty surrounding the events on Glienicker Bridge, one thing is clear. Pfrumpy was driving. Pfrumpy was responsible. This is what matters. By whatever means, magic or metal fatigue or whatever the hell you want to call it, it was Pfrumpy who drove that car off the bridge into the river where he and his two passengers drowned. Why?

— I'm still trying to find that out.

— Let me help you. One piece of information that was never included in the official police file was the pathologist's finding that Pfrumpy's wife had cancer. And that she was pregnant. Surprised? Add to this another piece of information I can now give you off the record, namely, that tests done in Montreal back in the early 1980s had established that Pfrumpy was sterile, probably as a result of sitting around in an unheated cave for so long, and you have the makings of a very plausible motive.

Peabody studied the plume of smoke rising from his cigarette.

— The two passengers in the car Pfrumpy drives into the river are his wife and her lover. Well. People who knew the household in Berlin shared by Pfrumpy with his wife and her lover, Babaji for one, yourself for another, describe their ménage à trois as having been all sweetness and light. It may have looked that way. But you're forgetting one thing, or rather, you're failing to take it into account, because you didn't know about it until I told you, the one truth about Pfrumpy that weathered all changes of life, embedded deep down in the skein of his nature, you know, *where the pig lives nobody knows about* — Pfrumpy was a bad loser.

— Yes, you said. But I never saw any evidence of that.

— Of course you did, only you shut your eyes to it for Christ's sake. Even after you have told me about the microscopic crack that Pfrumpy somehow figured out in the bridge and how he widened it until it was broad enough to drive a car through, you're still sitting there seeing all that sweetness and light. Well, to be frank with you, I think that's a load of baloney. You're admitting it was not an accident but a deliberate act, while at the same time you avert your eyes firmly from any motive for the deed. This was a *murder*, all right? Carried out by a man who, however good a face he put on the situation of having his wife's lover live in his house, took his revenge on both of them and got rid of himself at the same time. Pfrumpy could never lose. It hurt him to lose to Frank, who fathered the child Pfrumpy had failed to, and Pfrumpy never forgave him for that. He couldn't live with it. That's why he did what he did. Get this. *People don't change.* It's really not so difficult to understand. I don't ask you to believe what I believe, nor can you expect me to believe what you believe.

Out of a gaunt face that already seemed to prefigure his death mask Pea grinned bleakly at me across the room.

— How credible, after all, is your view of a paid-up Buddhist who not merely does not step aside on the Eightfold Path to avoid treading on the proverbial ant but kills *himself*, his *wife* and their mutual *friend*, let's face it, OK now, this was a *slaughter* — wilfully and with malice aforethought, as the law calls it, or, as people more commonly say: in cold blood? Eh?

I said:

— Well I don't know, Mr Peabody. You have put your case, but I'm not so sure. Let me put mine. Even if the world line leading up to Glienicker Bridge had become almost inevitable, as Pfrumpy would have been inclined to believe both by temperament and his training in Buddhist tradition, he did not want the cycle of events to be mistakenly traced back to him. He would not presume. He was of the chain, not at its beginning, just a small link in it, with an endlessness of oscillating links on either side. You might dismiss Pfrumpy's esotericism as baloney and call such an attitude superstition, but this was why Pfrumpy had been waiting patiently all the while for some impartial confirmation, a sign of outside approval, so to speak, from neighbouring links in the self-moving chain. Some time the chain will start rattling of its own accord, Pfrumpy told himself, and I shall be the one to hear it. These thoughts he shared neither with Wilma nor Frank. But that doesn't rule out that he had them. And bear in mind, Mr Peabody, what Babaji found upstairs in the library the morning after. Just imagine . . .

CHAPTER
21

When considering Heisenberg's 'strange kind of physical reality lying somewhere between possibility and actuality', not at the level of the microscopic events described by quantum theory but on the macroscopic level of human events, it becomes necessary to introduce the concept of *motivation* into a wave function describing the no less strange kind of physical reality lying somewhere between wanting and doing.

Although I knew Peabody's view of the events on Glienicker Bridge to be wrong, it did have an influence on mine. The severity of his judgement of Pfrumpy was at heart the severity with which Pea was judging himself. That was the chord struck in me when I heard Peabody use the phrase *where the pig lives nobody knows about*. He was talking about his own pig, not Pfrumpy's. Although I had trouble reconciling it with my own view, ridiculed by him as 'sweetness and light', in the light of Wigner's dictum that all the possible knowledge concerning an event, i.e. all the possible views of it, could be given as its wave function – and the wave function was after all the paradigm I was using to determine the events on Glienicker Bridge – I had no difficulty incorporating Peabody's interpretation into my own. The theory I was constructing already contained so many contradictions that a few more made no difference. The contradictions seemed to me more likely to strengthen than weaken a position based on the mediation of opposites, or what Pfrumpy had called the courtship of the poles in their eternal dance around the equator.

But Pea's anecdote about the unsmiling eyes (unsmiling eyes had been Frank's impression too) was for me a significant new factor in my reappraisal of Pfrumpy. It made plausible the stubbornness of purpose, the toughness of mind required to drive the car over the bridge, physically to *steer it through* the initiation site discovered by Pfrumpy and with which, I was quite sure, he had already been 'shining' long in advance.

That kind of unswervingness sounded true to character – Pfrumpy could have carried it out.

But to go on and say this was what he actually *did* was only feasible if one could at the same time explain satisfactorily *how* and *why* he would have done it – and here I was confident Peabody's version of Pfrumpy as a cold-blooded murderer entirely missed the mark, not to mention its failure to come to terms with what the technical survey commissioned by Peabody had deemed to be the virtual impossibility of driving a car off Glienicker Bridge.

What characterised the reality between wanting and doing was the process of transformation of an idea into a deed.

Given the enormous number of actions performed automatically in our daily lives, the idea usually lies so close to its execution that it is easily overlooked what an astonishing process, *in all cases*, the unconscious action no less than the conscious, such a transformation of idea into deed is.

The idea, you might call it a neurological impulse generated by a chemical factory, apparently something but really a sort of ghost, creates the energy, the energy the muscular co-ordination that plans and carries out the deed in a different world from the one in which it had been conceived – a process quite as mysterious as electromagnetic waves disturbing the vacuum and pulling negative energy electrons up out of it.

Such transformations may perhaps be more easily imaginable for a former inhabitant of a walled state, such as the one in which I was born and grew up, where monumental deeds are to be found everywhere, realised a hair's breadth away from their conception. The proximity cannot be overlooked because the discrepancy between the idea and the deed actually brings home to the inmates of walled states the extreme improbability of such monumental undertakings taking place under anything like normal circumstances, indeed their complete absurdity. This is because in a totalitarian state monumental ideas require no more than a stroke of a pen in order to become monumental deeds.

One looks at something all around one, a monumental fact such as a Wall dividing a city, or a fence enclosing an entire country, and despite its obvious familiarity from having seen it countless times, one still disbelieves the evidence of one's eyes, says to oneself: this cannot be.

How does such an idea become transformed into such a deed?

By diluting it in the process of delegation, creating separate authorship of the idea and the deed, the complete severance of the two.

Some such theory of severance might need to be adduced (having established with Einstein that we need the theory about what we are looking at in advance of being able to see it) to help solve the riddle of Glienicker Bridge.

One might for example imagine Pfrumpy in a trance-like state, in two minds, his physical system on automatic pilot, as it were, going through the motions of driving a car through a gap in a bridge, one part of his mind concerned with the execution of the deed, aligning the car with the gap in the balustrade and so forth, dissociated from the idea of the deed that had been pre-established in another.

In Pfrumpy's case, I did not believe anything of this kind had happened. I believed Pfrumpy had been seeking – right up until the very last moment when the car had already entered the experimental set-up on the bridge – a consensus with his two passengers regarding which of the two slits they should choose to pass through. The mere possibility of passing through one slit may have influenced the pull they felt towards the other. They would only go through the one because they might equally well go though the other. Had the wishes of Pfrumpy, Wilma and Frank not been synchronised the car would perhaps have continued across Glienicker Bridge and left it by the opposite exit. The mysterious moment of transformation when that choice was made, describe it with whatever figure of speech you will, synchronicity of entangled particles or collapse of the wave function or quantal transition from idea to deed, can only have been induced by an act of uniform consciousness on the part of all three of the participants simultaneously

Just imagine, I said to Peabody.

CHAPTER
22

On the morning of the wedding of Nick the Greek and his Lebanese bride Pfrumpy had come down early to put things in order in his library, where he found lying on the floor his copy of the Evans-Wentz translation of the *Tibetan Book of the Dead* he had been consulting in the course of his own work. The book must have slipped off the desk. He turned it over and found the pages open at one of the passages he had himself marked.

'The three chief symptoms of death are 1) a bodily sensation of pressure, 'earth sinking into water'; 2) a bodily sensation of clammy coldness as though the body were immersed in water, which gradually merges into that of feverish heat, 'water sinking into fire'; 3) a feeling as if the body were being blown to atoms.'

That was quite something of a rattle in the chain, hardly to be overheard, thought Pfrumpy.

Although he was not unprepared for it, had indeed been anticipating something like it, reading the passage he had himself marked, and realising it reproduced verbatim the images of sinking into water he had dreamed on the morning of his fifty-seventh birthday at Holm, had given even Pfrumpy something of a jolt. He did not tell Wilma or Frank about this episode either, just made a note of it in his journal and left the book lying open on the floor for Babaji to find on his return from Switzerland the following day.

When they left downtown Berlin, already an hour late, for the wedding of Nikos and his Lebanese bride on that October afternoon it was naturally Pfrumpy who was driving.

K. knew that Frank didn't care for driving, only drove when he had to, and as neither he nor Pfrumpy felt comfortable with Wilma's driving – fretful, said Pfrumpy, inspired though not always, Wilma admitted, while in Frank's opinion it shouldn't have been allowed on the roads – it was usually Pfrumpy who did the driving.

K. rather quaintly put this as a conjecture: 'Pfrumpy would have been driving' – less an expression of the probability of Pfrumpy driving than of K.'s habitual caution, as yet with no inkling of the deeper significance of Pfrumpy being in the driver's seat, of Pfrumpy 'doing the driving', driving as a figure of speech.

Pfrumpy had still said nothing, but he had been anticipating all along that in the end it would be up to him. Frank and Wilma, when it came to it, would be relying on him. Pfrumpy felt this pressure, but he was accustomed to it. He would come along on the excursion and just do the driving, unwinding the road, with a little help from Nagarjuna, like it was something that came out of the car, as if it was the car driving there that made the road. He could leave the road to attend to itself, up, down, left, right, whichever way it chose to go, not seek it by the turn of his own hand.

Heavy downtown traffic held them up en route for Zehlendorf. Nightfall was already coming on when they reached Glienicker Bridge. The road rose before them like a white scar in the gloom of the trees in the surrounding park. On the cobbled approach to the bridge, probably before the car actually rolled onto it, Wilma seemed to be disturbed by something. A flicker of unease, or what Pfrumpy took to be unease, just a shadow that flitted across her face, was apparently triggered by the giant hoarding she saw on the side of the road.

Pfrumpy stole a sidelong glance at her and noted the familiar signs that Wilma showed when she was agitated.

– Funny, where did that billboard spring from? I never noticed it before. Was it here last time we came? I've read that *slogan*, uhm, well, I don't know, *somewhere*, I mean not here, you know.

Pfrumpy said nothing.

– Siebenund – Frank, help me can you?

– *Siebenundfünfzig Jahre sind genug.*

— Fifty-seven years are enough?

— Right.

— Fifty-seven years of what?

— Well . . .

Frank began to explain as they crossed the bridge, but Pfrumpy could tell that Wilma wasn't really listening to what he said. She was listening inside herself, with a strained, puzzled expression on her face.

Pfrumpy pulled up outside an apartment block in Potsdam. I won't be a moment, said Frank. K. got out and Frank went with him into the building while the car waited at the kerb with the engine still running.

Wilma was still trying to make the connection. She sensed it there, lingering on the edge of her mind. It tried to push over into consciousness, but something was resisting it. It irritated her. She guessed it might have been Frank, lecturing her about the history of fascism, that had interfered with her own thoughts and prevented her from making the connection.

— It was fifty-seven years of something else, *quite* different from that business Frank was talking about, only I can't figure out what.

Frustrated, she looked across at Pfrumpy and noticed the eerily vacant look on his face that Wilma knew well, when he dropped out of ordinary consciousness and spontaneously entered samadhi. Wilma was not unused to it, but it still gave her the creeps. Pfrumpy could do this and at the same time continue on automatic pilot with whatever other activities. During the eight years in the mountains of Ladakh this was the kind of mental discipline Pfrumpy had learned from his Tibetan teachers. He could weave a mat, drive a car, cook a meal or repair some piece of equipment while the active, searching function of his mind was engaged in some quite separate train of thought. Wilma guessed what that train was and where it was headed. It was she herself Pfrumpy was concentrating on. It was Pfrumpy pushing against her, she was sure, resisting the admission of the already formed thought into Wilma's conscious mind.

— Pfrumpy.

Pfrumpy didn't respond.

– Pfrumpy?

Wilma put her hand on his arm.

– OK now, Pfrumpy. What's going on here? What's all this about?

Pfrumpy switched off the engine.

– You and me.

– You and me?

– What else?

Pfrumpy reached into his jacket and handed her the pocketbook.

– 'Fifty-seven years are enough.'

– But enough of *what*?

At which moment Frank got back into the car, bubbling over with the news he had just heard from K.'s supervisor, that K. had been offered an assistant lectureship, Wilma was distracted, Pfrumpy switched on the ignition and drove on to Holm without answering Wilma's question because Frank monopolised the talk and the conversation with Wilma was never resumed. Ten minutes after leaving the house in Potsdam the three of them arrived at the village hall in Holm, two hours late, where they found Nikos and his bride already married and the wedding reception in full swing.

As she danced in the wake of memories of that summer festival which seemed to go with the hall, first on the arm of the bridegroom, then with Frank, then with Pfrumpy, in the end all alone and with herself, Wilma wondered again: how had it been possible to forget one's own death? Only because of the strong habit you made of life. One got up in the morning, went to bed at night and got up again the following morning – and the world on either side of that interval of nothingness just put itself together again.

How mysterious!

So many dreamless nights survived without mishap, and then, what, falling down into a well of forgetfulness, from which you would never resurface?

You could be, as she herself was, terminally ill and still not believe in death. You believed in what was this side, the bright-haired arms and wrists of a short dark man playing some kind of Arabian lute, the beautifully formed lobes of his ears, neat little purses of flesh that paid their own way, detached from the surrounding skin of the face. A late butterfly had breezed in over their heads through the open hall door, fluttered up out of the dark auditorium and settled on him where he stood on the brightly lit stage. He was not here this time among the other musicians in the hall. Within moments of coming into the hall and not seeing him there on the podium regret passed rapidly into relief and back again to itself. But what other outcome could she have expected? He was not after all a friend of Nikos, just a professional musician who had been invited to the festival. Why would a Moroccan Jew be playing at the wedding of a Greek-Lebanese couple in a German village in any case? His band had been sponsored to come over for a gig at the local folk music festival and then gone back to Tangiers. That was it.

That was it!

What a bright sound, that instrument!

There it was again! Shedding notes that tinkled like drops of moisture on a terrace still warm from the day's sun.

They had a suite overlooking the harbour. Listen, Wilma said to Pfrumpy, there's a band out there somewhere playing, and they went in search of it, running down the crooked steep paths and flights of stairs to the sea front where the flickering sound seemed to be coming from, now here, now there, changing its location all the time and refusing to be pinned down. She had no complaints. He ran with her. He had been everything a man should be who was so much older than his young wife – guiding her, caring for her, supporting her when she often wavered, entering her younger spirit and being or at least seeming to be her like-minded companion without patronising or making fun of her.

Why then was all this still not enough?

How could she continue to miss him even when he was still there?

And in any case: enough of what? Was there something else that she had missed?

Pfrumpy and Frank, both of them still there during the harmless summer days at Holm before their lease expired in the fall, where the sheets smelled of the garden where they had been hung out to dry, and the scent of a wild rose bush flourishing on the wall under her open window would sometimes drift in over her in the middle of the night – why not enough, these pleasures and the happiness they briefly released in her, which lived only on the cusp of losing them, it was only under the threat of their extinction, of soon not having them, that she could be aware of having had them at all. The butterfly flew up and away, she had thought she wouldn't see it any more –

And then there it was, pumping its wings on the bright-haired wrist of the lute player where it had landed, someone she had met for just a few nights and would never meet again.

Absurd! How was such an absurd thing possible?

How possible?

Pfrumpy could sometimes see a way where Wilma saw none. Look, he said, taking his hands off the wheel as the car rolled slowly onto the bridge, no hands, it can drive itself. We make a left just ahead, Pfrumpy said, all right? It has to be left if it's not right. It can only be the one because it's not another. And still Wilma didn't see it, only Pfrumpy's shining. But when, in some foregone unspoken collusion with Pfrumpy, perhaps mindful of the latter's baffling admonition to Frank that Wilma's life was in his hands, a figure of speech he had never forgotten, Frank reached over her shoulder, as if something had just occurred to him, and gave the slightest of turns, a slight correction, to the wheel, setting the car on the slow traverse towards the exit at the middle of the bridge, Wilma clasped Frank's wrist and held it tight – in the spasm of the clasp, pulling abruptly down on the hand that held the wheel, suddenly Wilma saw it too, the butterfly rising brilliantly out of the dark chrysalis of the blight. The taste of happiness was only ever in the aftermath, in the aftermath was where it briefly lived and breathed, when whatever it was to which it owed its being, that thing from which it came, that thing was itself no more. 'Pfrumpy's bird is my butterfly,' she cried out with a painful sense of wonder – and they flew from the bridge.

NOTES

[1] Oral communication to author

[2] TAZ March 4, 1990

[3] TAZ March 9, 1990

[4] Oral communication to Wilma Pfrumpter

[5] The interdependence of two objects, however great the distance separating them. Entanglement is the translation of Verschränkung, a term coined by one of the founders of quantum physics, Erwin Schrödinger, whose thinking was deeply influenced by Indian philosophy. Allegedly, it was an ancient Sankhya-Hindu paradox which, jazzed up with some technology, became famous as Schrödinger's Cat Paradox (see footnote 35).

[6] For an introduction to Bell's Theorem see, §11.0,

[7] 'The pattern built up, by pulsing the gun many times and photographically recording the electron flashes, (occurs) over a region which gets bigger, rather than smaller, when the holes by which we try to determine the electron trajectory are reduced beyond a certain magnitude. There is a still greater surprise when the hole is replaced by two holes close together. Instead of these two holes just adding together, an 'interference pattern' appears. *There are places on the screen that no electron can reach, when two holes are open, which electrons do reach when either hole is open* (Observer's italics).'

[8] Author's italics

[9] In conversation with Heisenberg, as related in the latter's autobiography, Einstein remarked: 'The possible, what might be expected, is an important element of our reality, which alongside actuality cannot simply be ignored.' (*Der Teil und das Ganze,*)

[10] 'Many physicists were convinced that the apparent contradictions belonged to the inherent nature of atomic physics' (Heisenberg, *Quantentheorie und Philosophie*)

[11] Pauli, *Aufsätze und Vorträge über Physik und Erkenntnistheorie*

[12] 'Its essence may be expressed in the so-called quantum postulate, which attributes to any atomic process an essential discontinuity, or rather individuality, completely foreign to the classical theories and symbolised by Planck's quantum of action.' (Niels Bohr, writing in 1928)

[13] Just how different the new physics was from Newton's universe can be glimpsed in the hypothesis of the existence of anti-matter put forward by the younger-generation P.A.M.Dirac. 'With the idea of anti-matter,' announced Dirac, 'we have rather to change our views about what is meant by a fundamental particle, or an elementary particle. Particles can be created just out of some other form of energy, such as the energy of electromagnetic waves. We may have electromagnetic waves *disturbing the*

vacuum and pulling up one of the negative energy electrons, and then we have created an electron and a positron, which get created simultaneously.' (Observer's italics). A kindred thought had been expressed in different language by the Indian Buddhist Nagarjuna two thousand years earlier. 'Phenomena which are void simply originate out of phenomena which are void.' Verse 4 in *Verses on the heart of Dependent Origination*

[14] In their conversation in Einstein's Berlin apartment Einstein told Heisenberg: 'One day you are going to have to explain to me what the atom is doing when by emitting light it passes from one stationary state to another.'

[15] A discussion of the striking analogies, however, between leaps of atoms from one energy state to another and the transitions of the mind between states of meditation induced by yoga, is presented in §19.

[16] For a detailed treatment of string theory see B. Greene, *The Elegant Universe*

[17] See §11 for further discussion.

[18] The idea of electron spin was introduced by Uhlenbeck and Goudsmith. It is loosely analogous to the spin of a ball and it was already implied by Pauli's Exclusion Principle in the mid-1920s. It was denoted by O with only two possible values, + or − 1. For J.S.Bell's description of spin see footnote 63.

[19] 'The quantum postulate implies that any observation of atomic phenomena will involve an interaction with the agency of observation not to be neglected. Accordingly, an independent reality in the ordinary physical sense can neither be ascribed to the phenomena nor to the agencies of observation.' (Niels Bohr, writing in 1928)

[20] For a detailed treatment of Bell's Inequalities see §11.

[21] E.g. Alexandrow and Blochinzew. 'Among the different idealistic trends in contemporary physics, the so-called Copenhagen school is the most reactionary.' The article quotes Lenin's unsurprising conclusion that the new physics 'is but another confirmation of dialectical materialism.' *Sowjetwissenschaft* 6 (4), 1953

[22] Bohr's reputation for mysticism may have been nourished by the impenetrability of his writings. Just what his pronouncements mean remains controversial to this day. J.S.Bell, for one, admitted that he was baffled by Bohr. The choice of the yin-yang double symbol for inclusion in his coat of arms can be taken as a reliable indication of Bohr's spiritual allegiance to the perennial philosophies of the East rather than the West.

[23] Agricultural Production Co-operative

[24] Heisenberg, *Quantentheorie und Philosophie*

[25] Heisenberg, *Daedalus* (1958)

[26] Compare Wittgenstein's axiom 'Man sieht nur, was man weiß' (You only see what you know)

[27] Similar to a bubble chamber

[28] *Der Teil und das Ganze*

[29] Heisenberg's choice of words here, 'eine gewisse Ungenauigkeit,' *a certain imprecision*, reflects both the inherent paradoxes of the quantum mechanics view of the world and the dilemma of the Observer in his attempt to be a reliable witness of so called reality

[30] Heisenberg explicitly acknowledged the debt to Einstein in his essay *The Development of the Interpretation of the Quantum Theory*. 'I tried to solve the problem of how to pass from an experimentally given situation to its mathematical representation, by inverting the question, that is, by the hypothesis that only those states which can be represented as

vectors in Hilbert space can occur in nature or be realized experimentally. This method of solution....had its prototype in Einstein's special theory of relativity.' *Niels Bohr and the development of physics* (1955)

[31] Author's italics

[32] *Speakable and unspeakable in quantum mechanics*

[33] i.e. the atomic object under investigation

[34] E.P.Wigner in *The Scientist speculates*, ed. I.J.Good

[35] 'One can even set up quite ridiculous cases. A cat is penned up in a steel chamber, along with the following diabolical device (which must be secured against direct interference by the cat): in a Geiger counter there is a tiny bit of radioactive substance, so small, that perhaps in the course of one hour one of the atoms decays, but also with equal probability, perhaps none; if it happens, the counter tube discharges and through a relay releases a hammer which shatters a small flask of hydrocyanic acid. If one had left this entire system to itself for an hour, one would say that the cat still lives if meanwhile no atom has decayed. The first atomic decay would have poisoned it. The wave function of the entire system would express this by having in it the living and the dead cat (pardon the expression) mixed or smeared out in equal parts.' Erwin Schrödinger, 'Die Gegenwärtige Situation in der Quantenmechanik', in *Die Naturwissenschaften 23* (1935). It might be added that researchers at the Time and Frequency Division of NIST at Boulder, Colorado made the first observation of quantum entanglement of four particles. They confined four singly ionised beryllium atoms in an electromagnetic trap so that they were spaced along a line. They then used lasers to cool the atoms to near absolute zero and forced them all to be in the same spin state. Laser light then entangled the atoms by exploiting their mutual electrical repulsion, creating a superposition of all four atoms being *both spin-up and spin-down simultaneously*. This can be seen as another small step (four atoms instead of one) toward affirming the principle of superposed quantum states illustrated by Schrödinger's example of a cat both dead and alive at one and the same time. *(Nature, March 16, 2000).*

[36] Author's parenthesis in italics

[37] Costa de Beauregard, *Quantum paradoxes and Aristotle's twofold information concept*

[38] Babaji's oral communication to author

[39] Rosencranz , Humphreys, Barrington et al in *Parapsychology Review*, July-August 1970

[40] See for example 'Calamity Jane at the National Press Awards', Toronto *Globe and Mail*, October 10, 1979

[41] There is no scientifically researched evidence for the assertion that the multiple-role tasking so characteristic of women may be connected with a broader archetype. One of its obvious differences from the compulsive male monotype is that man born of woman's womb expends so much of his energy in efforts to re-enter it, an option not available for women, giving them more freedom to exercise a greater variety of others.

[42] The term 'American-Indian' was used by Pfrumpy when describing his first meeting with Wilma in an interview with Observer. For full transcript of text see the Pfrumpter Foundation Archives in Montreal (hereafter abbreviated as PFA/M to distinguish it from a second collection in New York with the code PFA/NY). The correct term today would be First Nations People. In fact, Wilma's 'American-Indian features' reminded Pfrumpy of the Tibetan features of the women he had encountered

in the Himalayas, which perhaps accounts for the force of that first impression of Wilma in the library.

[43] Italicised parenthesis added by author

[44] Fritjof Capra, *The Tao of Physics*. Compare T.V.R.Murti's elucidation of the position of Nagarjuna in *The Central Philosophy of Buddhism, a study of the Madhyamika System*: 'It might be thought that though there might be difficulty about the precise moment or place of the commencement of the motion, the distinctions of time into past, present and future, and of space, into the traversed etc. are available. Not so; without motion, these spatial and temporal motions distinctions too cannot be made. The nerve of the argument is stated thus by Nagarjuna: 'Distinctions of space (and of time) into the traversed (past), to be traversed (future) and that which is being traversed (present) are dependent on the arising of motion itself' (Mulamadhyamakakarika 2. 14) for that alone serves as the dividing line. But the rise of motion itself is inexplicable without these very spatial and temporal distinctions which it engenders. The essence of the Madhyamika standpoint in this regard would be that the divisions of past, present and future etc. are of some ubiquitous substance and cannot be understood without this underlying entity.' In Nagarjuna's philosophy, this ubiquitous substance anticipates the quantum field of modern physics, the 'continuous medium which is present everywhere in space.

[45] The following material is a summary of a videotaped deposition made by Peabody to author in December 1998. See the Peabody Papers in PFA/M.

[46] ibid.

[47] Shakespeare, *King Lear*

[48] PFA/NY

[49] ibid.

[50] Bohm, *The undivided universe: an ontological interpretation of quantum theory*

[51] ibid.

[52] In both excerpts the underlining is Pfrumpy's

[53] 'Jedes Ding besteht durch seine Grenzen und damit durch einen gewissermaßen feindseligen Akt gegen seine Umgebung. Damit ist es nicht von der Hand zu weisen, daß die größte Anlehnung des Menschen an seinen Mitmenschen in dessen Ablehnung besteht.' (Musil, *Der Mann ohne Eigenschaften*)

[54] PFA/NY Even in this most personal of letters, the influence of Nagarjuna on Pfrumpy's thinking is unmistakable. Compare the following assertions from the *Mulamadhyamakakarika* in McCagney's translation. 'Going and a goer do not exist as separate thoughts. Where going does not exist, where then will there be a goer?' (Chapter 2) and 'The seer does not exist either separated or not separated from seeing. If the seer does not exist, where is the seeing and the seen? (Chapter 3)

[55] Pfrumpy once shocked a dinner party with his pronouncement that the Jew persecuted by the Germans was the Jew in themselves. Whether he was himself Jewish is an open question. In the light of Peabody's anti-Semitism, coupled with a self-confessed jealousy of Pfrumpy that bordered on hatred, his claim that Pfrumpy's mother was Jewish must be treated with caution.

[56] PFA/NY

[57] Most interactions in physics appear the same when reflected in a mirror. But not all. When an atom emits a neutrino, the neutrino spins in the same direction –

anticlockwise. Reflected in a mirror, however, the neutrino would always spin clockwise. This asymmetrical property of matter was discovered in 1956 by Tsung Dao Lee and Chen Ning Yang. They noted that the symmetry could be restored, however, if a parallel universe existed in which neutrinos rotated in the opposite direction – clockwise – to that in our world.

[58] 'The contradiction in the applications of old contrasting conceptions (such as particle and wave) is only *apparent*...it would be most satisfactory of all if physics and psyche could be seen as complementary aspects of the same reality' – 'The influence of archetypal ideas on the scientific theories of Kepler' in C.G.Jung and W.Pauli *The interpretation of nature and the psyche* (1955)

[59] 'At night there is no light, and so no colour, but by this we know what light is, by darkness. Opposite shows up opposite as the white man the Negro; the opposite of light shows up what is light; hence colours are known by their opposites. God created pain and grief to show happiness through the opposite. Hidden things are manifested thus. ' Jelal u-din Rumi, *The Masnavi*. This is strikingly similar to a remark attributed to Buddha. 'This so called element of light is known through its dependence upon darkness.'

[60] Franz Kafka, *Die Metamorphose*

[61] Bell's 'note' was pronounced by the physicist H.P.Stapp to constitute 'the most profound discovery of science' – quite a claim. Some of the reasons why Stapp should have attributed such importance to Bell's Theorem are presented in §11.

[62] Discussion of this argument was broached in §5,

[63] 'It helps to know how physicists think of particles with 'spin'. In a crude classical picture it is envisaged that some internal motion gives the particle an angular momentum about some axis, and at the same time generates a magnetisation along that axis. The particle is then a little like a spinning magnet with north and south poles lying on the axis of rotation. When a magnetic field is applied to the magnet the north pole is pulled one way and the south pole is pulled the other way. If the field is uniform the net force on the magnet is zero. But in a non-uniform field one pole is pulled more than the other and the magnet as a whole is pulled in the corresponding direction. The experiment in question involves such non-uniform fields – set up by the so-called Stern-Gerlach magnets.' Bell, *Speakable and Unspeakable in Quantum Mechanics*

[64] For non-mathematicians it remains an elusive concept, but it has been graphically illustrated by University of Toronto physicist David M.Harrison in terms that can be understood by the layman. Starting with the Inequality expression: Number (A, not B) + Number (B, not C) >= Number (A, not C) Harrison comments: 'In class I often make the students the collection of objects and choose the parameters to be: A: male; B: height over 5'8"; C: blue eyes. Then the inequality becomes that the number of men students who do not have a height over 5'8" plus the number of students, male and female, with height over 5'8" but who do not have blue eyes is greater than or equal to the number of men students who do not have blue eyes. I absolutely guarantee that for any collection of people this will turn out to be true.' But while this inequality will always be fulfilled within classical systems, in the domain of quantum mechanics it is violated.

[65] Feliks Edmundovich Dzerhinsky was in 1917 appointed head of the new All-Russian

Extraordinary Commission for Combating Counterrevolution and Sabotage, or Cheka, which became Soviet Russia's secret police

[66] Bohm, D. and Aharonov, Y. (1957), 'Discussion of experimental proof for the paradox of Einstein, Podolsky and Rosen,' *Physical Review 108*

[67] Transcript of author's interviews with Babaji , Ref. 46/95, PFA/NY

[68] Our evidence for Pfrumpy's prior visit, or rather visits to Glienicker Bridge are the photographs he took of it, apparently on different occasions

[69] A well-to-do residential neighbourhood in Berlin. The pale blue notebook is among the PFA/M papers

[70] The word occurs twice in the blue notebook, the second time in the interrogatory phrase 'bridge for stone?' The stone referred to here may be the pebble Pfrumpy brought back from Ladakh. Its use as an aid to meditation is explained in §16.2,

[71] Recorded in Pfrumpy's private papers, PFA/NY

[72] Frank's recollection of this scene was related to author not long after the event. He had a remarkable memory combined with a no less remarkable mimic gift. Thus he did not merely paraphrase things that a person said but reproduced them as if he had become that person himself. The style of the person mattered as much as the gist of what they said. Some of Pfrumpy's characteristics are reproduced here, the idiosyncratic pauses in mid-sentence, an eerie use of conventional phrases dislodging the familiarity one thought they had, for example the hard-to-place 'Now that you are here' in Pfrumpy's opening sentence.

[73] Though not to Lawrence Peabody. For his reading of Pfrumpy's eyes see §20.2

[74] PFA/NY

[75] Letter from C.G.Jung to W.Pauli, in *Wolfgang Pauli und C.G.Jung, Ein Briefwechsel 1932-1958*

[76] Wilma Pfrumpter Colleetion, Museum of Photographic Art, Montreal

[77] Orfeu Negro (1960)

[78] 'I dreamed I was buried alive and Wilma brought me back above ground.'

[79] In the *gTum-mo* practices, which result in the production of psychic heat, the adept has to concentrate upon the element fire in order to heighten his own body temperature, maintaining his body warmth regardless of how cold it is around him. There are many well-documented cases of yogis doing *gTum-mo* in the Himalayas, melting the snow on which they are sitting.

[80] In a footnote to the headline we might have wished to add that there was a deviation of around 20% from the maximum theoretical value of 1, but we figured this was all attributable to the imperfect working of our instruments, chromatic dispersion effects in the interferometers and so on. Correcting for such deficiencies, the correlation rate of entangled particles in yes-no choice situations 6 kilometres apart was 100%.

[81] Professor Q. has never been seen or heard of since. But the idea he broached at the Twin-Photon Luncheon about introducing relativity to the experimental set-up, resulting in two particles both being measured prior (depending on the point of view) to the measurement on the other, was suggested independently some years later by Antoine Suarez and tested by Nicolas Gisin's group of applied physics at the University of Geneva. Q. was proved wrong. The photons continued to show quantum correlations, suggesting they were not sensitive to space or time and could not be explained by a causal chain of events within the nonlocal quantum realm. 'Time does

not seem to pass here' was Suarez' lapidary conclusion in his paper *Entanglement and Time*.

[82] Words underlined in Pfrumpy's copy of the book, PFA/M

[83] The radiation regarded as the best evidence for the Big Bang theory of the origin of the universe.

[84] In this context, note J.A.Wheeler's apodictic quantum position: 'No elementary phenomenon – whether now or in the earliest days of the universe – is a phenomenon until it is an observed phenomenon' *Quantum theory and measurement*. This raises the interesting question: who in the earliest days of the universe was there to observe it?

[85] H.J.Stapp, *Quantum Ontologies*. The Latin word *potentia* from which Stapp's expression derives was first introduced by Heisenberg as part of his 'strange kind of physical reality, lying somewhere between possibility and actuality '.

[86] The seriousness of *gTum-mo* itself is not in doubt. Harvard Medical School Professor Herbert Benson studied monks in the Himalayas who used *gTum-mo* to raise the temperatures of their fingers and toes by as much as 17 degrees and lower their metabolism, or oxygen consumption, by 64%. *Harvard University Gazette, April 18, 2002*

[87] Compare J.S.Bell on the double-slit experiment: 'Although each electron passes through one hole or the other (or so we tend to think) it is as if the mere possibility of passing through the other hole influences its motion and prevents it going in certain directions.'

[88] See for example Targ, *Miracles of Mind*. From 1957 to 1965 Dr Bernhard Grads at McGill University in Montreal investigated the ability of healer Oscar Estebany to affect distilled water in sealed containers (ampoules). These contained a lightly saline solution (1%) that was used to water plants. Estebany agreed to treat by thought some of the saline-filled ampoules before they were used for watering, and the result was that the plants watered with this solution grew significantly faster. This seems to suggest that a mental influence over the state of a nonliving system, such as water, implies direct psychic interaction with a part of the physical universe.

[89] Sanskrit: Desa-bandhas cittasya *dharana*.' 'Concentration is the confining of the mind within a limited mental area.' Patanjali *Sutras*, Section 3

[90] *Ibid*

[91] *Ibid*

[92] *Pratyaya*, rendered here as 'seed', is a technical Sanskrit word meaning the total content of the mind

[93] i.e. into the surrounding 'outside' world

[94] Compare the 'blurred impression' of Heisenberg: 'We had always just told ourselves that the path of the electron in the cloud chamber was something one could observe. But perhaps what one actually observed was rather less than that. Perhaps all one could perceive was just a discrete series of imprecisely determined locations of the electron.'

[95] I.K.Taimni, *The science of yoga*

[96] §9, Section 3, Patanjali *Sutras*

[97] Taimni, *ibid*

[98] §12, Section 3, Patanjali *Sutras*

[99] Taimni, *ibid*

[100] Western scholars date Patanjali as having lived at some time between the ninth and fourth century BCE, Hindu pundits some thousands of years earlier than that